# "Neither of us is any good at relationships, I guess."

"It's not us, Mallory. It's just that everyone else has unreasonable expectations. We work long, hard hours." Cliff frowned. "But I like going out with women. I like dating. I like—"

"Sex?" she asked sweetly. "Are you saying you can't go without it?"

"I happen to like women. So sue me," the lawyer in him responded.

Her smile faded. "Maybe you just need to have an affair."

Cliff sighed. "Every time I date, the woman pulls the same old your-work-means-more-to-you-than-I-do routine. I haven't even made it to first base with anyone in ages."

She nodded. "You know there's a solution to all this. We merely have to find someone to…to…"

"Have sex with occasionally?" he inserted silkily.

She tipped her chin upward. "Yes. Good clean sex." Mallory took a deep breath. "Why don't you and I have an affair?"

## Dear Reader

Have you ever concocted the perfect plan? You know what I mean: you decide you'll just get that particular job, then you'll head up that high-profile project, bringing it in under budget and on schedule, of course! That will naturally lead to another promotion, and, before you know it, you're the head honcho.

At least, that's the way the plan goes.

Or maybe you'll just clean out that front hall closet, the one you have to lean against to shut the door. Then, while you're at it, you might as well get rid of the kitchen floor's waxy yellow build-up, rewire your house and convert your attic to a charming vacation getaway complete with whirlpool and excercise room for less than fifty dollars.

I got to thinking about plans—and reality—and I realised that, for most of us, real life has a nasty way of interfering with our ambitions. So that was why I had my hero and heroine construct their own plans to build perfect lives, get their perfect jobs and conduct a *perfect* affair. As a writer, all that perfection was just too good a target to pass up.

And wasn't there something about the best-laid plans…?

Happy reading!

*Marissa Hall*

To Joyce Winter,
the big sister I always wanted

*First published in Great Britain 2000
Harlequin Mills & Boon Limited,
Eton House, 18-24 Paradise Road, Richmond, Surrey TW9 1SR*

© Maureen Caudill 1999

ISBN 0 263 82050 5

*Set in Times Roman 10½ on 12¾ pt.
01-0101-37651*

*Printed and bound in Spain
by Litografía Rosés, S.A., Barcelona*

# AN AFFAIR OF CONVENIENCE

BY
MARISSA HALL

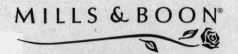

MILLS & BOON®

# 1

MALLORY REISSEN fiddled for the fourth time with the glass of ice water by her plate. Why had she given in to Mark's demands and agreed to this Sunday brunch?

It wasn't the restaurant. She'd frequented La Grande Passion's Sunday buffet on a regular basis since she'd moved into a nearby condo complex three years ago.

It wasn't the weather. She and her date sat in a small nook on the restaurant's terrace in bright San Diego spring sunshine. At the other table in the nook, intent on their own conversation, sat her handsome neighbor Cliff Young and his current girlfriend.

It wasn't even the company. Mark was an attractive, entertaining man—most of the time.

When he wasn't haranguing her about her work habits.

''Mallory, you've got to put things in perspective. You're never on time for any of our dates. And that's not counting that you break half of them because your boss wants you to do a 'little something' extra.''

A flush tinged Mark's face, giving it a pettish, un-attractive quality.

"I was on time today, wasn't I?"

"Yes," he snapped. "The first time ever. Should I give you a medal?"

She put down her fork and tried to ignore the tightening of her stomach. God, she hated this. How many times had she gone through the same argument with other escorts? Fifty? A hundred?

"No," she said. "A simple recognition that I'm not always—"

He didn't let her finish. "The only reason you were on time today was because I told you that we were through if you weren't!"

"Hush! This is a public restaurant." Too late. Mallory's gaze had already been snared briefly by Cliff's at the next table. His date sat with her back to Mallory and Mark's table, and Cliff was facing them.

"Do you think I care?" Mark said without lowering his voice. "I'm a good catch. I could have practically any woman in San Diego, and you're too busy fussing with your cameras and makeup to notice."

Mallory sighed. "Mark," she said as gently as she could manage, "as a television news anchor, cameras and makeup are part of my business. It's what I do." She touched the pristine pink linen napkin to her lips to hide their wry twist. She'd heard this complaint a hundred times, too. "You knew about my job before you asked me out the first time."

"Yes, but I didn't know you'd made your job into some kind of obsession. And a full-time one at that."

Damn. Men always wanted more from her than she could give. Didn't any man understand that a woman in the television-news business had to work twice as hard, be twice as good, to command respect?

To be a success, to become someone even her parents would admit had done well, she had to break out of the local news market onto the national scene. That big break hovered just around the corner. She could feel it. She'd already received a few feelers from one of the networks. Nothing substantial, of course, but still...

But to grab that opportunity when it finally presented itself, she had to prove herself better than all those other local newspeople.

She had to be the best.

And being the best meant always being ready to cover a breaking news story, wherever and whenever it happened. That always-on-call status sometimes— often—meant broken dates, late arrivals, damaged egos whenever she tried to have a relationship with a man.

None of them ever understood how important it was to her to be a success. None ever realized that any personal relationship—even a lover—must always take second place to her career. And rightfully so. The only way she knew to get ahead was to put job and career at the very top of her priority list.

Those priorities had worked so far, though she had left a string of broken relationships and lost friendships scattered behind her.

Frustrated, concerned she would say something to Mark that would sever the few threads remaining in their friendship, she rose and manufactured a smile. "I'm going to get a plate from the fruit table."

She lingered at the artistic display of exotic fruits to avoid returning to the argument Mark seemed determined to pick. She reached for a luscious strawberry, but the tongs she held were trembling so much she nearly dropped the berry.

A warm masculine hand closed over hers, steadied the tongs, and helped her put the berry on her plate. Startled, she looked over her shoulder, prepared to jerk away, only to relax when she realized the hand belonged to Cliff.

"Thanks." She reached for another strawberry along with a dollop of sweetened whipped cream— her fatal weakness—and again his hand kept hers from fumbling.

He took the tongs and lifted two or three succulent berries to her plate. "Enough?"

"Yes." More grateful than she felt comfortable admitting, she studied the display of fruit, mainly to keep from having to meet his gaze. She didn't want more to eat—she knew she would have a hard time swallowing the fruit already on her plate.

"Trouble with your date?" Cliff asked in an undertone.

She started to lie, then stopped herself. What was the point? Cliff had to have overheard much of her argument with Mark. Besides, in the three years they'd lived next door to each other, she'd come to count on him as a casual but very real friend. She had shared more in-depth conversations with him than with anyone else she could name.

Something about Cliff inspired confidence. It was one reason he was a terrific lawyer, she supposed. But long ago she'd learned to stifle the occasional pang of attraction that surfaced and to concentrate on building a platonic friendship with him.

He seemed to be doing the same, never giving even the slightest hint that he wanted anything more personal from her.

"Yeah," she admitted, dragging her mind away from Cliff and back to their conversation. "Mark's not very happy with me right now."

"Why? Have you been two-timing him?" He put the question so smoothly that it took her a moment to take offense.

"Of course not!" She turned to look at him fully.

"I barely have time for one relationship. When would I find the time for another?"

He shrugged, and plucked a juicy green kiwi slice for his own plate. "Women cheat all the time."

"Not me." Mallory glanced over her shoulder. From this angle she could see his date's face. She thought she recognized her as an actress currently starring in a production downtown at Spreckel's Theater. "If you ask me, your friend doesn't look too happy, either."

Cliff grimaced and added a spoonful of raspberries to his plate. A questioning brow asked if she wanted some too, and she nodded automatically.

"She's not. In fact, I think Suzanne and your guy could well be singing the same song."

"I don't understand."

"Wasn't Mike—"

"Mark."

"Oh. Well, wasn't Mark complaining that you spend too much time working? That you break dates because of work commitments? That you don't spend enough time with him? That you willingly sacrifice your social life if something needs to be done at work?"

Mallory's jaw dropped. Hastily, she shut it again. "How did you know?"

He hunched a shoulder to subtly indicate his date,

who was now tapping her fingers on the tabletop. "Sounds just like what Suzanne says to me."

Their eyes met in mutual understanding. Mallory knew that Cliff was one of San Diego's hottest defense attorneys. He had once confided over coffee that he planned to be the youngest partner ever in his law firm, the most prestigious in San Diego. She knew enough of his schedule to understand that sixty-to-eighty-hour workweeks were typical for him.

Just as they were for her.

"I'm sorry," she said softly.

"It happens." He glanced over at their tables as he snared a couple of muffins. "I guess we've both stalled too long."

Mallory turned and saw Mark swallow the last of his champagne cocktail, get to his feet, and stalk off. As he passed the fruit table, his glare should have incinerated her on the spot, though he didn't say a word.

Right behind him came Suzanne. She sashayed up to Cliff, ran her crimson-tipped fingers along his jaw, and gave him what had to be a stinging pat.

"See you, Cliff," she said. "Next time you want to get together, give me a call. If I'm not doing anything that night—" her tone indicated that counting coat hangers in her closet would be preferable "—maybe we can see each other."

She sauntered away, snaring every masculine glance in the room.

Mallory looked down at her plate of fruit and over to their two empty tables, then glanced up at Cliff. "What do you want to bet both our respective dates stuck us with the checks?"

CLIFF SMILED, relieved to see the hint of laughter lurking in Mallory's eyes. While Suzanne had been jabbing his ego with her subtly snide barbs, he'd found himself straining to overhear as much as he could of the conversation at the next table. The tension between Mallory and Mark could have supported a span of the Coronado Bridge.

Although he'd never tried to date Mallory himself, her relaxed manner and sympathetic smile made him count her as one of his few friends. He rarely allowed people close enough to be called friends.

The lure of that friendship was strong enough that he'd deliberately trained himself not to think of her in a romantic way. It wasn't that he wasn't attracted to her—he was. But he didn't want to ruin the one so-far-successful relationship he'd ever forged with a woman.

He walked with Mallory back to their seats. Sure enough, each table had an unpaid check for two outrageously expensive buffet brunches. He set his plate of fruit and muffins on his table, thought better of it, and carried it and his check to Mallory's table.

"We might as well finish the meal together, don't you think?"

"Well...I'm probably not very good company right now."

"Haven't you ever heard that misery loves company?" Without waiting for a response, he slid into the chair across from her. "Besides, I'm sure the restaurant would appreciate having an open table. Didn't you notice the line of people waiting to be seated?"

She fingered her fork but made no move to pick it up. "We could just leave. Then they'd have both tables for other parties."

"And waste a brunch that's going to cost each of us well over fifty bucks? Are you kidding?" Cliff wasn't really joking. Although he could spend money with the best of them, he made sure he got good value for his dollars. When you grew up thrift-shop poor, you didn't waste your pennies. Or in this case, you didn't waste your twenty-dollar bills.

With a smile that spoke eloquently of Mallory's reviving spirits, she said, "You're right. Let's at least get a good meal out of this disaster."

After a few moments, Cliff picked up an enormous blueberry muffin and buttered it. "Was it such a disaster for you?"

Mallory cocked her head in a characteristic position he'd seen her assume many times on the nightly news. A surprised note entered her voice. "You know, I don't think so. Mark obviously didn't understand me very well." She paused. "What about Suzanne and you?"

He shrugged. "Same thing." He put down the muffin and leaned forward, striking his best Henry Higgins pose. "Tell me, Mallory, why *can't* a woman be more like a man?"

"What? I don't know what you mean."

"This whole thing with Suzanne. I've been through it a dozen times. I invite a woman out for a date. We have a pretty good time. Then, sooner or later, I have to work late on the night she wants to go to the opera. Or I can't take her to some party because I've got a court date I have to prepare for." He leaned back, his point made. "Women always try to trap a man into doing something that jeopardizes his job."

"Women? What about men? Do you know the number of times I've had to cancel a date because of a breaking story, only to have my escort give me hell for not adapting to his schedule? Or how many times men have backed off as soon as they realize that I don't work a simple nine-to-five shift?" Mallory's cheeks glowed as she warmed to her theme.

She glared at him, food forgotten, and he glared right back. Dammit, he was just trying to point out…

A laugh surfaced and he relaxed against the back of his chair. "You know what we're saying? We're two of a kind, you and I. We're both paying the price."

Her smile glimmered then faded. "Yeah. Neither of us is any good at relationships I guess."

"It's not us, Mallory. It's just that everyone else has unreasonable expectations. We work long, hard hours. We have to be dedicated to our jobs if we want to get ahead. We're not the ones with the problem. It's everyone else." He took a huge, satisfying bite of his buttered muffin.

She swallowed the last of her strawberries. "So you're implying that we both have to put personal relationships on hold until after we're established in our careers. You're going to make partner within a few years and I'm going to be at one of the networks. Until then, we just have to cool it."

Cliff frowned. He couldn't see any flaw in her reasoning, but that didn't mean he had to like her conclusions. "But I like going out with women. I like being around them. I like dating. I like—"

"Sex?" she asked sweetly. "Are you saying you can't go without it?"

Pugnaciously, he stuck his chin out. "I happen to like women. So sue me."

Her smile faded. "It sounds like you just need to have an affair with someone."

"Like who? I'm telling you, every time I begin to think about getting involved with a woman, she pulls the same old your-work-means-more-to-you-than-I-do crap. I haven't even made it to first base with anyone in ages." Suddenly aware that he'd admitted more than he'd intended, he shut his mouth.

Sneaking a peek across the table, he saw a genuine smile flirting along the edge of her mouth.

"Mallory Reissen," he said accusingly, "if you don't make it big-time as an interviewer, it's not for lack of talent. How the hell did you get me to admit so much about my love life?"

"Or lack thereof?" Her smile transformed into a smirk. Definitely.

"Or lack thereof." Funny, he didn't even mind her knowing. A suspicion snuck into his head. "And I'll bet your love life isn't any more, uh, satisfying, is it?"

Her eyes met his and the smirk faded. "No. Men don't like to hang around the edges of a woman's life. They want to be front-and-center all the time. I can't give them that, so…"

"Front-and-center? That would drive me crazy. I don't need—or want!—a woman center stage in my life. All I want is an occasional comfortable evening with a woman who understands that my work is very important to me. Is that so much to ask?'' He paused, then admitted, ''With maybe some really great sex thrown in. Just to keep things interesting, you know?''

She cocked her head again. ''If I ever find a man willing to take less than a full-time commitment from me, I'll be sure to tell you all about it.''

He finished his muffin in silence while she polished off the last of her raspberries. He didn't really want to wait for years to share intimacy with a woman. He didn't want to make a major commitment, either, of course. But that didn't mean he had to live like a monk.

Did it?

Mallory interrupted his morose thoughts. ''You know, there's a solution to all this. We merely have to find partners who understand going in that all we really want is a pleasant, healthy physical relationship. Neither of us wants a family right now. We don't want someone to cling. We just want someone we can, um…''

''Have sex with on the odd occasion?'' he inserted silkily.

She tipped her chin upward. ''Yes. That's exactly what I mean. We just want an affair that's got some good, clean sex—and there's nothing 'odd' about it. What's so bad about that?''

He smiled and snagged a lonely slice of papaya off

her plate. ''Nothing. All you have to do is tell me how we go about finding such amenable partners.''

''Well, we could advertise, I suppose.'' She propped her elbow on the table and put her chin in her hand. ''Isn't that the growing thing in the nineties? Going the personal-ad route?''

''That's dangerous. Especially for you. All kinds of crazies answer those ads, and with you being a public figure and all—it's just not safe.'' He repressed a shudder at the thought of what might happen if some nut found her.

''Well, what do you suggest?''

He considered her question carefully. No doubt about it, they were both in the same pickle. ''Maybe we could…help each other out,'' he said slowly, feeling his way.

''Help each other? How?''

''Well, you understand women better than I do. And I probably understand men a little better than you. What makes us tick, and all that.''

''So?''

The hint of a plan nudged forward. ''Maybe you could help me find a woman who wouldn't be such a clinging vine. And I'd help you find a man who wouldn't mind your working late.''

His idea had merit, he decided. It was a good plan. Surely she would be able to tell him which women he could count on to understand his situation. She could make up a list of potential candidates. Then he could talk to them, see them, and decide which one would do. And he could do the same for her. He probably knew half a dozen men who would be pleased to take her out any time she was available.

His plan was perfect. It was simple. It was logical. It was surefire.

"It would never work." Mallory's blunt comment punctured his rising spirits.

"Why not? It seems simple enough to me."

She gestured impatiently. "Because it won't, that's all. Women fool other women as easily as they fool men. And with you as the prize…"

His ears almost physically pricked up at that. "What about me as the prize? What's wrong with me?"

"Nothing. That's the point. Women would crawl all over you—or me—to get into your bed. You're young. You're making good money and will be making even more in the future. You're good-looking. You're sexy. What's not to like?"

"You think I'm sexy?" Why had that one phrase stuck in his head? He tried and failed to burst the bubble of attraction that surfaced.

"Of course I do! Who wouldn't? That's my whole point." She brushed a strand of hair back behind her shoulder. He'd always liked the fine golden strands, especially when she wore it down. On most of her television broadcasts, she tamed it into some kind of sleek bun.

"I don't get it." Not for the first time, he imagined that smooth blond hair running through his fingers—then shook the thought away. She was his *friend,* dammit. Not some babe to hit on. "What's so bad about being sexy?"

"Nothing—except that it makes it all but impossible to figure out who's sincere and who will decide after the fact that she wants more."

He considered that point. Yeah, he could understand that women might line up to leap into bed with him. Of course, he hadn't ever noticed them doing it in the past, but it could happen.

Sure it could.

Of course, the same was true of her. She had the looks—striking cheekbones, translucent skin, great curves. She had a sex appeal that could lure men with a smile. Yeah, his problem in identifying candidates for her wasn't a matter of coming up with a long enough list of possibilities. Instead, he'd be hardpressed to prune the list to manageable proportions.

And guys did lie to other guys, too.

He pondered the unexpected complexities of his potential task. The click of Mallory's champagne goblet meeting the table interrupted his thoughts.

She took a deep breath. "Rather than look for other partners for each other, why don't you and I have an affair?"

# 2

ONCE THE WORDS popped out, Mallory wished for nothing more than to pull them back. How had she found the nerve to suggest that she and Cliff have an affair—together! She opened her mouth to deny she'd made the suggestion, but it was too late.

"You mean, you—and me?" he asked.

His words took a bite out of her ego. "You don't have to sound so astonished. I mean, some people consider me—"

He waved her to silence. "Yes, of course. But I never thought about you and me, uh, like that."

"If you're not interested, we could go back to considering your plan."

"No! I mean, it's not that I don't want to. I'm just kind of surprised you suggested it."

She leaned forward, pushing her plate to one side. "Look, Cliff, we know each other reasonably well."

"Yes, I guess we do."

"And what we know, we like."

"Uh-huh." His face adopted a definite wary look.

"Neither of us wants ties or commitments right now—we can't afford them if we're going to build our careers."

He nodded with certainty. "That's for sure."

"And both of us are prime targets for people who want to latch on to our success. At least, I know I am, and I'd be willing to bet you are too. Right?" She waited for him to challenge her assumption.

"Yes," he admitted. "Suzanne constantly asked me how much I made, and if I represent any of the Hollywood types that hang around in La Jolla."

Mallory allowed herself just a trace of satisfaction. "That's what I thought. The point is, we both know we're safe from that kind of thing with each other. I don't need you to advance my career, and you don't need me."

"That's true, too."

His hand captured hers and a trickle of heat warmed her skin. Startled, she pulled her hand away. This was no time for distractions.

"The key thing is that you want a partner to enjoy an occasional evening with—without having to worry that she's going to cling and demand too much of your attention. I want the same thing." She shrugged and smiled. "Sounds to me like we're made for each other."

He drummed his fingers against the table. "You've got a point. Maybe we are."

"Best of all, we live next door to each other. We don't even have to bother with the usual dating stuff. When we want to get together, all we have to do is go next door."

"Another excellent point."

Was she making sense? She thought so, but couldn't be sure. Still, there was one last thing she had to be clear about....

"I just had my physical last month." She didn't let the blush searing her neck interfere with her blunt announcement. "I'm, uh, perfectly healthy."

To her relief, he took no offense. "Me, too. Mine was just a couple of weeks ago. And I'm very careful about sex. I always have been." A boyish grin lightened his serious expression. "Wanna swap medical histories?"

His humor eased her embarrassment. "I don't think so," she said. "I trust you."

He clasped her hand again and this time she didn't pull away. "That's what we're really talking about here, isn't it? Trusting each other not to make demands neither of us is capable of meeting?"

"Uh-huh." She rotated her palm so her fingers interlaced with his. "Trust. Respect for each other's career. And a little old-fashioned sex."

"Not too old-fashioned, I hope!" His boyish grin was back and she smiled in response.

Still, as they raised their glasses in a mutual toast

to their pact, for some odd reason she felt a stab of concern as she looked into his eyes.

*What had she done?*

She put down her glass and gathered her courage to keep her voice calm and level. "So we're in agreement?"

"Yes." His smile was half predatory and half reassuring—and totally seductive. "We're going to have an affair that's guaranteed not to interfere with our careers. None of this love-and-happily-ever-after business. Just two people out to have a good time together with no strings."

"Right." Why did it sound so cold when he summed it up that way? She certainly hadn't felt cold when she'd proposed it.

"One thing, Mallory."

"What's that?"

The dark, seductive tone had left his voice, making it deep and utterly serious. "If you want out of our agreement at any time, just say so. You don't even have to give me a reason. Just tell me it's over and that will end it."

The gray of his eyes sharpened to silver. It was obvious that this stipulation was very important to him. She didn't know if he'd been burned with other girlfriends who'd clung too long or if something else triggered it. Either way, he wanted a way out of the relationship.

An escape route.

She didn't want to agree to his implied request for the same assurance. For some reason she couldn't quite define, the thought of articulating the easy-out nature of their agreement made her shift uneasily. It made everything seem so…sordid. Her throat closed, and she swallowed hard to clear it. His gaze held hers with its utter sincerity. He didn't look as if he thought she'd proposed anything unsavory.

Her agreement popped out before she could stop it. "That's fine. And the same for you. If you want to leave anytime—" her voice caught and she had to swallow hard to continue "—just tell me. No problem."

*What have I done? What have I done?*

He visibly relaxed. "Good. Then I guess we really do have an agreement."

"Should we put it in writing?" she asked, trying to keep the cynical note out of her voice. "After all, you being an attorney and all…"

He cocked his head and tapped his cheek with one finger. "No," he said slowly. "We're not contemplating any commingling of funds or assets, so I don't think it's necessary."

He'd actually considered it! How could he!

She almost stabbed him with her fork before she saw a suspicious twinkle in his eye. "You're teasing me, you rat."

Suddenly, she felt a lot better about their new arrangement. His humor reminded her that she could have fun with Cliff—and fun was something her life sorely lacked. Fun, sex, companionship—what more did she need?

*Nothing,* she told herself firmly. *I don't have time for more.*

"I was just kidding you a little bit." He tipped up her chin and gave a wicked grin. "Couldn't you tell?"

"I can now. And I warn you. You won't catch me off guard so easily again."

"No? You sure of that?" His eyes teased her unmercifully.

"I'm sure," she promised. "But you might want to watch out yourself."

While their banter continued, Mallory realized she was genuinely enjoying herself, more than she could remember doing for years. His teasing-flirting-enticing manner reminded her of exactly why she'd conceived of their plan in the first place.

Surprisingly, she couldn't wait to find out if the other benefits of their arrangement would be equally enjoyable.

She put her napkin beside her plate and shoved her chair back from the table. Now, with excitement fizzing in her veins like the bubbles in her champagne, she could hardly wait to get him to herself. ''Why don't we leave now? We can go home and…''

But nothing would let her finish that thought with his eyes on her. Eyes that held an unmistakably salacious gleam.

''Good idea,'' he drawled. ''By all means, let's go home and…''

YET, DESPITE her earlier eagerness, when they walked out of the restaurant, Mallory's doubts resurfaced. She would never have believed a five-minute car ride could generate so much tension. Neither she nor Cliff said a word as he expertly backed his gold Lexus sedan out of its parking space, turned onto the street, then almost immediately turned into the condominium parking lot.

During that brief time she envisioned a hundred ways to handle the situation.

*My bed or yours?* No. Too blunt.

*In the mood for a little whoopee?* Too dated.

*Cliff, you're very sexy. How about coming over to my place and I'll show you how much?* Too overt.

*Wanna get naked?* Too raw.

Dozens more comments flitted through her mind, but none appropriate for a woman who had just asked a man to have a sex-only, no-strings affair. Nothing in her life had prepared her for a situation quite like this.

With a start she realized that Cliff had pulled the car into his garage and turned off the engine.

"Having second thoughts?"

She shivered. She'd known the man for three years, so how come his voice suddenly sent goose bumps up and down her spine? From somewhere deep inside her, she dredged up enough courage to meet his eyes. "No. No second thoughts."

*Liar!*

No, I'm not, she assured her screaming conscience. I'm having twelfth or thirteenth thoughts. My second thoughts came and went minutes ago.

"I'm glad." His hand touched hers for a moment, then he opened the car door and got out. Too soon, he walked around the front of the car and opened her door.

Silently she accompanied him to the front door of his town house. It looked like a mirror image of her own. *Get a grip, kiddo. You wanted exactly this. So why are you so nervous?*

Because it's different! She wanted to scream the words. She wanted to make a run for the sanctuary of her home. She wanted to forget she'd ever mentioned such a stupid idea. She wanted to lean against Cliff and have him tell her everything would be all right.

She wanted...

The door stood open, and he stood aside, waiting for her to enter. ''Do you want to come in now?''

Was that break in his voice from nerves too?

For the first time since they'd left the restaurant, she took a good look at him. His hair, a deep glowing auburn in the sunlight, had an unusual disheveled look. A fine quiver tickled one cheek and his Adam's apple bobbed as he swallowed deeply. No question about it, he was as nervous as she!

The realization calmed her, and she tried to reassure him with her best smile. ''Sure.''

He ushered her into the living room that bore a surreal, reversed resemblance to hers. But while her unit's decor featured elegant eighteenth-century cherry furniture, Cliff's had modern brass and glass mixed with two huge burgundy-leather sofas and modern art prints on the bleached-oak paneled walls.

''A glass of wine?'' His voice had a slight catch that betrayed his nervousness.

She took a deep breath and walked close to him, breathing in the spicy aroma of man and aftershave. ''Don't bother, Cliff. This isn't about seduction, you know.''

''It's not?'' He had to swallow before the words came out. She noticed, however, that his hands had come to rest on her hips.

''No.'' She raised her hands to unbutton his designer knit shirt. "It's about each of us getting what we want from the other."

His hands moved restlessly over her tailored slacks. "And what is it you want from me?"

Any trace of nervousness had utterly vanished from his voice, leaving a dark seduction that rippled through her. It set her heart thumping and froze her hands at their task. She breathed deeply and her head swam from the rich luxury of his scent. Her hands went to work, tunneling under his shirt to the warm muscles of his back.

"I just want you," she told him. And she did. She wanted his charm. She wanted his teasing. She wanted his humor. She wanted his companionship.

Most of all, right now she wanted his lean, hard body.

He smiled. "And I want you." Gently he lowered his head until his lips barely touched hers. Breathing the words into her mouth, he added, "More than anything, I want you."

His lips finally descended fully on hers in a gentle kiss that nonetheless carried the fire of passion. That first touch was both tentative and assured, the kiss of a man who knows he has the time to taste and the inclination to savor.

Mallory let herself relax against him. Her arms tightened around his back, moving restlessly against his sinewy strength. She breathed in his intense, manly scent, part spicy cologne, but mostly pure Cliff. Giddy, she savored the combination of sensations.

Their mouths touched, separated, touched again. Each contact lasted a fraction longer. Each separation was incrementally briefer. His hands roved over her back until one lodged at her nape, holding her head at the perfect angle to deepen the kiss.

Only when she gasped for air did he release her, pressing his forehead against hers. Even while concentrating on regaining her breath, she noted that his lungs strained as hard as hers. She moved one hand from his back and around his side until it hovered over his heart. The thumping beat beneath her palm confirmed his excitement.

''You pack a wallop, Mallory,'' he whispered. His mouth tenderly explored her temple and the corners of her eyes. ''How come you never told me about this before?''

She froze. ''This?''

''Your heat. Your fire. Your passion.''

She relaxed and let her hand do its own exploring. He had the most marvelous chest! ''Maybe you never asked me?''

''Can't imagine why not. Can you?'' A thread of humor laced his voice. ''I mean, here I've been, cold and lonely right next door to you. And you, hard-hearted woman that you are, never said a word about being hot enough to warm the coldest nights and the loneliest bachelor.''

He accompanied his accusation with at least a dozen more of those tender, tempting kisses. She tilted her chin to give him better access to a particularly sensitive spot. "I confess, Counselor. Guilty as charged." His tongue generated a spear of heat blazing through her, making her voice breathy. "I throw myself on the mercy of the court.''

He paused just long enough to send her an approving smile. "Perfect response, Ms. Reissen. And definitely a fascinating idea. The prospect of you throwing yourself on top of me leaves me barely able to stand upright.''

Mallory's wandering fingers burrowed through the silky hair on his chest and found the raised pebble of his nipple. Her lips curved in triumph when his breath caught.

"You think I'm properly contrite for my crime, Counselor?''

He sent her a mock frown. "Maybe not. I think I need to see more of your willingness to atone for your felonious ways.''

"You mean—'' She didn't have to ask him to clarify his pronouncement. He was already busy unbuttoning her silk blouse and spreading it with a jerky movement. Her bra received equally brief attention before its front clasp released and the two sides spread apart.

He stared at her uncovered breasts for a long moment, before raising his eyes to meet hers. His voice deepened to a husky note. ''I mean you're the most beautiful thing I've ever seen.''

Her mouth dropped open in surprise. Unlike their earlier banter, she couldn't find the slightest hint of humor in his quiet words.

''Cliff…''

''Mallory,'' he mocked gently, ''didn't you expect a compliment or two along the way?''

She smiled with seductive intent, her hands busily tackling his belt buckle. ''I hadn't thought about it, I guess. But it's very nice, Counselor. Smooth. I think I'm beginning to understand why you hotshot lawyers are so slick.''

''You do, hmm?'' His words were muffled because his mouth nibbled her ear, sending quivers through her. He whispered directly into her ear, ''Wanna find out how come they call me the office hotshot?''

His erotic promise turned her spine to a river of fire and conjured images that burned her breath in her lungs. He pushed her blouse and bra off her shoulders, letting the garments fall to the floor. While her hands surged through the dusting of hair on his chest, his palms covered her breasts and pebbled nipples. He bent and closed his lips over one breast.

Mallory's breath stopped, though her heart thundered. Every sense concentrated on the liquid flame of his mouth against her flesh. Blood rang in her ears, a musical, insistent tone that echoed over and over and...

"Cliff—" She struggled to get the word out through lungs that barely remembered how to function. "Cliff...wait."

"Hmm?" His mouth released her nipple and drifted over the fullness of her breast toward the other aching mound. "Just a minute."

The ringing hadn't stopped. "Cliff. Wait." With every bit of strength she could muster, she pulled his head away from her. The frustration glittering in his eyes almost made her groan, but she persisted. "My pager. It's beeping."

It took a moment, but she saw the arousal fade in his face and awareness replace it. He loosened his grip on her enough to allow her to step away. It wasn't easy when every atom in her wanted to step closer, but she managed.

And with that slight distance, sanity returned. She scooped up her blouse and pulled it around her, not bothering with the bra, which she stuffed into the pocket of her pants. She took one shaky breath, then another, before reaching for her purse to retrieve the persistent device. A familiar number displayed on the screen. "It's—" she cleared her throat of the final traces of passion "—my boss. I have to call him."

Cliff waved her toward the phone on the table. His eyes still held lingering flickers of arousal, but he said nothing while she absently buttoned her blouse.

With the closing of each button, Mallory felt more in control, more professional. By the time Stanley Rosen, the station's news director, answered the phone, she could speak with her usual crisp tones.

Less than two minutes later, she hung up and turned to face Cliff. He, too, had repaired his appearance, stuffing his shirt back into his pants and rebuttoning it. "I take it you have to leave?" he asked before she could say anything.

"Yes." Just looking at him heated her blood—but she had no time for that now. "There's a major story breaking at Camp Pendleton. Stan wants me to come in and anchor the coverage."

If she were with Mark, she knew he'd be protesting that the marine base north of the city always had some "breaking story" or another. But Cliff merely nodded. "I understand. Do you need me to do anything for you?"

She wanted to feel happy that he was letting her go to work so easily. She ought to feel happy. But disappointment lingered. "I'm sorry about…this." She gestured vaguely to indicate the passion that had exploded between them and the interruption that had killed it too soon. "We'll have to start our, um, association later."

He reached her side before she realized he'd moved. "Don't worry. We'll pick up where we left off another time."

Despite her own hormones singing in her veins, she smiled at him. "And will you remember where we were before the interruption?" she asked softly.

He gave her one hard, lingering kiss before escorting her to the front door. "Count on it."

She left quickly, refusing to look back at the temptation of his farewell.

HOURS LATER, Cliff still blinked in wonder that Mallory Reissen had actually propositioned him!

With his sensual plans for the day ruined, he had decided to make use of the afternoon as he did most Sundays—by working. He'd changed into his favorite grungy sweats and parked himself on the couch in his living room, with a stack of paperwork covering the coffee table in front of him and Mozart filling the air.

As he mulled over the complex briefs needed for a client meeting the next day, he had to admit that she'd definitely come up with the best solution to both their problems. She'd looked serious, a little earnest, even...sweet while she calmly and logically explained why some hot nights in the sack together would solve both their problems.

He shook his head. He found it hard to imagine he'd ever thought of Mallory as "sweet," but there it was. Her hopeful-but-please-don't-notice expression reminded him of sneaking kisses from Barbara Sue Denton behind the bleachers at a pep rally.

Of course that was before Barbara Sue's parents convinced her that dating a kid from the wrong side of town was only one step away from being with a leper.

He hadn't thought of Barbara Sue in years. Last he heard, she'd been married and divorced twice and was on the prowl for husband number three. He spared a moment of silent thanks that said husband would never be him, then returned his attention to his paperwork.

Despite his concentration, his soon-to-be-consummated affair with Mallory sparked a glimmer of anticipation and tightened the fit of his normally loose sweats. Kissing her had been an exercise in pleasure he hadn't anticipated. Not even the charming, half-shy uncertainty in her eyes when he'd bared her breasts compared to the luxury of her kiss.

He regretted the untimely interruption from her beeper—a lot. He wished she'd been able to stay, though he understood the demands of her career had left her no choice. If she had stayed, he knew he'd have had her upstairs and naked in his oversized bed within minutes. The details of what he planned to do to her, with her, for her, simmered in his mind.

It was going to take him hours and hours to go through every step of that envisioned scene. Then he would start all over again.

Yes, he thought as he shifted once more to accommodate the hardness that showed little sign of abating, sex with Mallory was going to be spectacular.

Their affair could well incinerate them both with passion, but he had no compunction about diving headlong into the flames. He wanted her more than he could ever remember wanting another woman.

And he intended to have her—very soon.

# 3

On Friday night, Mallory dabbed a final puff of powder on her nose, grabbed her purse, and started for the door of her office. She had talked to Cliff this afternoon when he called to arrange a late dinner—late because she couldn't leave work until after she'd anchored the six-thirty evening news, which usually meant leaving the station somewhere around seven-thirty. They planned to grab a quick meal, then go home and finally get their fledgling affair off the ground.

She could hardly wait. After the untimely interruption on Sunday afternoon, the prospect of starting an affair with Cliff offered an even more enticing reward for surviving a long workweek.

A quick glance at her watch showed the minute hand creeping ever closer to the twelve. She was late, of course. Why was she never able to get out of the station at a reasonable time?

Firmly putting her work out of her mind, she was flicking off the office lights when the electronic chirp of her telephone halted her in the doorway. She stopped, debating whether to go back and answer it or just let whoever was at the other end assume that she'd already left for the day.

A second chirp, then a third convinced her. With a disgruntled sigh, she flipped the lights back on and returned to her desk. Without sitting down, she picked up the phone.

"Mallory Reissen here." At this time of night she didn't care if her voice was a little curt.

"Mallory, glad I caught you." The voice of her agent boomed through the receiver, so she pulled it away from her ear. "I wasn't sure you'd still be at the station. Should've known you were too dedicated to have left already."

She grimaced, glancing again at her watch. Cliff would be looking for her at the restaurant very soon. "What is it, Lenny? I was just on the way out the door."

Another hearty chuckle blasted her ear. "Well, you know that tape I sent to the network guys last month?"

"What about it?" Suddenly she was *very* interested in what her agent had to say. Thoughts of the date with Cliff faded.

Lenny summed it up in two words. "They're interested."

Her breath caught, and she collapsed into her chair. "Tell me this isn't a joke."

"No joke, kid. They haven't made a final decision, of course. But you've definitely made it onto their short list. They told me that much already."

Visions of success danced before her eyes. She had to take three deep breaths before she could get any words out. Dozens of inarticulate questions buzzed around her head, but the only one she could think to ask was, "Did they tell you anything more about the project?"

"Not really. But they did dangle one carrot."

Lenny always had a sense of the dramatic. He was going to make her ask.

"What carrot?"

"Are you sitting down?"

"Yes," she said impatiently. "What carrot?"

"It's for prime time."

Long moments passed. For once in her life Mallory could think of absolutely nothing to say. "I don't believe it," she finally whispered. "Prime time. Are you *sure?*"

"Scout's honor, kid." Again Lenny chuckled. "Looks like we're headed for the big time."

"But they haven't made up their minds yet, right?"

"That's right. They'll be talking to you and two or three other candidates over the next few weeks.

It's up to you to convince them that you're not just someone on their short list—you're the only person on their final list.''

"I can do that," she vowed.

Twenty minutes later, having rehashed the entire situation with Lenny several times before hanging up, she finally arrived at the small Thai restaurant where she had arranged to meet Cliff. Despite being a solid half hour late, she practically floated to the table on winged feet. The words "network prime time" filled her head almost to the exclusion of anything else.

As she sat down at the table where he waited, she apologized for her tardiness.

"Don't worry about it," he said, handing her a menu. "I was a little late myself. I take it things got a little crazy at work?"

She nodded. "I'll tell you about it later. Have you ordered?"

"Nope. I was waiting for you."

To her relief he didn't show the slightest sign of disgruntlement. This arrangement really was going to work out, she thought while she scanned the menu. He understood when business interfered with their plans and made her a little late for social stuff. The thought cheered her even more.

They ordered a simple meal of pad Thai rice noodles with shrimp and settled back to talk. Mallory explained about the last-minute delay leaving the station and he congratulated her on her opportunity.

"Of course, it's way too early to celebrate. It could be months before they actually make up their minds. And these new projects can be cancelled before they even get on the air." She tried to inject a note of realism to keep herself from getting too excited too early.

"Yes, but things do look good."

"That they do." Putting down her chopsticks, she lifted her glass of wine in a silent toast.

This was one of the best parts of their infant relationship, she realized as they enjoyed their dinner. She could talk to him about her work without worrying that he would think her overly ambitious or unfeminine. His congratulations on her successes tasted sweeter than any dessert. She tried to remember when any man had displayed such a reaction to a professional coup. She couldn't think of a single occasion since she'd begun to make her mark at the station.

She smiled at him over a cup of steaming ginger tea. "I've really been looking forward to tonight," she confessed. "I'm sorry things didn't work out on Sunday, but it's going to be even better now. We— I really have something to celebrate."

Cliff shifted in his seat. "Yes. Well."

But she interrupted him. "But we've been talking

about me all through the meal. What about you? How's your work going?''

With precise care he positioned his cup on the table and didn't meet her eyes. ''Busy, of course.''

''I know what you mean,'' she said when he failed to expand on that comment. Something was bothering him, but what? ''Is anything wrong at work?''

He smiled too quickly. ''Of course not.''

She believed that just about as much as she expected the sun to rise over the Pacific some morning real soon. On the other hand, she didn't want to pry if he didn't want to talk. ''Maybe we should go home,'' she suggested. *And maybe you'll feel more like talking once we have some privacy.*

''Uh, that's the problem, Mallory.''

She froze, her chair half-shoved back from the table. ''Problem?'' Had he changed his mind about their agreement? Was this dinner together merely a way of telling her he didn't want a relationship with her after all?

*Or was he a lot angrier about her lateness this evening than he'd let on?*

''Cliff, if this is about my being late,'' she said carefully, ''we did agree that—''

His surprised look cut her off. ''Why would I be mad about that? I know your job entails unexpected demands.''

''Oh.'' She paused, still balanced on the edge of

her chair, afraid to either continue or abort the move-ment. "So what's the problem?"

He took her hand. The warmth of his palm against hers melted the frozen lump inside her and let her relax again against her chair. "I just feel like I got you out here under false pretences. I know I implied we'd go home from here and…well, anyway, I'm afraid that's not going to be possible tonight."

"Why not?" Whatever his message, she didn't un-derstand it.

His words came out in a rush. "Mallory, I have to go back to work tonight after we leave here."

"On a Friday night?" she asked blankly.

"Yes." His gaze searched her face while he ex-plained. "The firm is going to take on a major case—the Bartlett murder trial—and the client is coming to the office tomorrow morning to talk about it with us. I've got to review everything for the meeting. I'm up for a position on the defense team—and if I get it, I'll be the only nonpartner included."

Fiona Bartlett was a much-married socialite who had—according to the press accounts—shot her fourth husband when she caught him in bed with another woman. The husband and his lover were killed, and Fiona allegedly wiped the gun, cleaned up, and left the house to go to their Palm Springs home. When the police arrived there to notify her of her husband's demise, she had put on an impressive show of histrionics. Ten days later, after a highly publicized investigation, she had been charged with two counts of first-degree murder.

The case promised to be nothing less than a circus. Women's groups claimed that if Fiona indeed had done the crime, it was because her husband abused her and drove her to murder. The prosecutor insisted Fiona planned the entire thing with cold-blooded calculation. Fiona professed her innocence and great love for the slain husband everyone knew she planned to divorce.

Meanwhile, the public gobbled up every salacious detail of the Bartletts' opulent, sensual life-style. In fact, Mallory's news reports offered updates on the case nearly every day.

Immediately she understood the implications of his words, and her palm gripped his fiercely. "Cliff, this could be an incredible break for you. Surely the senior attorneys must think very highly of you to consider including you on a case like this!"

As if he suddenly realized that she was congratulating him, not condemning him for a disappointing evening, he relaxed and let a huge grin surface. "I've been told that my participation in a successful resolution of this case would definitely result in 'positive appreciation from the powers that be.' I think that means a partnership could well be in the works."

She couldn't resist planting a smacking kiss on his cheek. ''Wonderful! I'm so pleased for you.''

''But I'm afraid we're going to have to put off our evening together until another time.'' Genuine regret shone in his eyes, which went a long way toward soothing any frustration that lingered.

She waved the comment away. ''Of course. You're right. You have to go back to work and prepare for the meeting tomorrow.''

They left the restaurant and Cliff walked her to her car. When she had opened the driver's door, his hand stopped her from getting in. ''You know, I really hated having to tell you our evening had to be canceled. What a relief to know you understand.''

Mallory turned to face him, only to find herself all but surrounded by his arms and the open car door. ''I do understand, Cliff. It's a tremendous opportunity for you. And I'm glad you're not angry about my being late tonight.''

He tipped his head, considering. ''Well, about that...don't you think I should get some kind of reward for being so sympathetic?''

Even in the distorted illumination of the parking lot lights, she could see the gleam of sensual teasing in his eyes. ''What did you have in mind?'' The breathiness in her voice surprised her.

''Maybe...a kiss?'' His mouth lowered, just a whisper away from hers.

She hesitated a moment to savor the anticipation, then lifted her face just enough to make contact. Her lips molded to his and clung, focusing her attention on the moist warmth radiating from him.

Her arms slipped around his neck. With an equally smooth motion, his arms moved around her waist and pulled her into the curve of his body. Automatically she fit herself against him, savoring his heat and strength.

He lifted one hand and used a thumb to nudge her mouth open, and his tongue took immediate advantage of the opening, swooping inside her mouth in a territorial claim she had no wish to deny. Her tongue dueled with his.

By the time he broke the contact just enough to rest his forehead against hers, both were almost breathless.

"Wow," Cliff whispered.

"Wow, yourself." Her hands loosened, to slide to his shoulders. "Why didn't you tell me about your earthshaking skills?"

"Me? I thought it was you."

With a compliment like that, how could she resist? She stretched on tiptoe to kiss him again. She'd always believed good behavior should be rewarded, she thought hazily while his lips captured hers and took charge of their kiss. And this was reward enough—or almost enough.

This time it took the raucous blare of a horn to separate them.

Reluctantly stepping away from her, Cliff's hands lingered on her waist before dropping to his side.

Mallory tipped her head and peered up at him. A few deep breaths steadied her voice. She hoped. "You've got to go back to work. Remember?"

"Yeah." He didn't move.

"Work? The meeting tomorrow? Remember?" If he didn't move, she knew she couldn't. Not while he was standing there looking as sinfully tempting as a box of Godiva chocolates.

Finally he shook his head and took another step away. "You're dangerous, woman. You know that?"

"I could say the same about you."

He traced a shaky finger down her cheek. Automatically she tilted her head into the slight pressure. "I'm likely to be tied up all day tomorrow. What do you think about continuing this sometime Sunday?"

"I think that's a wonderful idea." At last free of the spell he wove so effortlessly, she slid into her car. Her keys rattled loudly as she blindly stuffed the right one into the ignition. Habit was a wonderful thing sometimes. "Go to work, Cliff. I'll see you Sunday afternoon."

But as she drove away she could see him standing in the parking lot watching her leave.

HOURS LATER, Mallory still hadn't gotten to sleep. Fantasies of being with Cliff invaded every speck of consciousness. Every time she dropped off to sleep, heated dreams of the two of them, entwined in ecstatic explorations, reappeared. Her sheets twisted into knots and her stomach churned from the need writhing inside her.

When the telephone trilled at 3:27, she was wide awake, staring at the black ceiling. Hastily, she grabbed the receiver. Was Cliff home? Was he burning for her as she was for him?

"Hello?" She winced at her own eagerness.

"Hi, Mallory. It's Mother."

Mallory's desire dissolved like the morning fog under a July sun. Another glance at the illuminated clock in her bedroom confirmed the time. She was probably the only person in America whose mother would call her in the middle of the night.

"Hi, Mother. How are you so early in the morning?"

"Fine, dear. Uh, early?"

"Yes. *Early.* It's three-thirty out here."

"But it's six-thirty here and you're three hours ahead, right?"

Mallory gave up. For a woman with a Ph.D. and an acclaimed academic career, her mother never could keep straight the time difference between the

East Coast and the West. "That's all right. Is anything wrong?"

"Oh, no. I just heard from your father. Enjoying himself immensely. He's in the middle of that concert tour. Eastern Europe, I believe. The Europeans so *appreciate* classical music, you know."

"That's nice. Did he ask you to contact me?" Mallory couldn't help the stiffness that iced her voice. Her parents maintained an apparently happy two-career marriage in which neither partner spent more than a few weeks a year in the same city as the other. It worked well for them, but not as well for Mallory. After her grandmother died when Mallory was twelve, she was brought up by expensive nannies and spent much of her time in boarding schools.

"Of course, dear. He is always very interested in how you are doing."

*I've heard that lie my whole life.* "I'm fine. Was there something you needed?"

"Well, yes, there was."

Disappointment tightened Mallory's stomach before she deliberately forced it to relax. She should be used to this by now. "What can I do for you, Mother?"

"I'm going to be on the West Coast in a couple of weeks. I'm meeting with Jonassen up at Stanford to prepare for this summer's dig. I thought you and

I might get together for a lunch or something while I'm out there.''

''Mother, Stanford is in the Bay Area. It's six hundred miles from San Diego.''

''Oh.''

Damn her for sounding disappointed! Of course Mallory gave in. Again. ''I'll see what I can do, all right?''

''That's fine, dear. I was cleaning out some of your grandmother's things and found a few items to give you. I thought it would be just a little cold to put them in a box and mail them.''

*Cold,* Mallory could deal with. A token maternal visit chilled her more than polite formality at arm's length.

''I see.'' Mallory scribbled down the dates and times of her mother's trip and promised again to try to arrange to meet with her while she was here.

Conversation over, Mallory tried to recapture the dreams that had kept her company all night long. Better the physical frustration of wanting Cliff and not having him than dealing with the lifelong frustration of wanting a parent who simply couldn't be bothered.

CLIFF FRETTED with anticipation until Sunday afternoon finally arrived. By the time he opened the door to Mallory's knock, he could barely restrain himself to a single, sizzling kiss. "The barbecue's hot. The salmon steaks are marinating in the fridge. Let's go to bed."

She actually giggled. "What kind of a greeting is that?"

Leading her out to the patio at the back of his condo, he said, "An honest one?" He gave his best Snidely Whiplash leer.

She settled comfortably into a padded patio chair, propped her feet on a convenient stool, and waved him to his cooking duties with a grand gesture. "Don't distract me, slave. I've survived a very hard week, and I am here to be waited upon."

Obediently, he opened the gas grill. "Well, I've certainly raised waiting to a fine art after this week."

"As in waiting for me?"

He snatched a quick nibble behind her ear as he handed her a glass of iced sangria and a huge bowl of salad fixings. "Of course, I mean you. But while you're waiting to be fed, could you toss the salad?"

She smiled and agreed, but he noticed a fine tremor in her hands as she took the bowl.

While he fussed with the grill, they chatted about their work. But silently, he pondered the quiver he'd seen. Now that he looked at her, he noticed the dark circles under her eyes—artfully disguised by makeup, but present nevertheless. What the hell was wrong?

When he caught her stifling a third yawn, he said, "You have had a long week, haven't you? Anything wrong?"

She shook her head. "I just haven't been sleeping well."

*What's wrong, Mallory? Why aren't you sleeping?* Everything inside him wanted to ask the question, but he hesitated. Would such a question be considered unwanted interference? Too intrusive? If she was simply working too many hours to have time for sleep, would she assume he was criticizing her?

A sudden glimpse of the pitfalls of their career-friendly agreement kept him silent. No doubt as they settled into their new relationship, such issues would disappear, he assured himself as he turned the salmon on the grill. They would find a way to work things out.

The doorbell interrupted his silent, unconvincing argument. "I'll be right back," he promised with a smile. "Keep an eye on the salmon for me, all right?"

Long strides took him to the front door. He had every intention of ejecting his untimely caller—posthaste. But once he opened the front door a crack, a size-twelve, sneaker-clad foot jammed it the rest of the way open. Then the foot was followed by a tall, muscular frame and a shock of black hair.

"Lemme in, Cliff."

"You already seem to *be* in. It's nice to see you. Are you ready to leave yet?" Subtlety accomplished nothing with Todd Sinewski, Cliff knew. His best friend, accountant, and sometime handball buddy simply didn't recognize the concept. It merely rolled off his hide like water off a suntan-oil-slicked beach bunny.

"Aw, c'mon, buddy. I got problems."

"Too bad. Maybe you can solve them somewhere else."

"Nah. You've got a way with babes. Tell me what I'm doing wrong."

Before Cliff could refuse, Todd launched into a detailed account of his latest dating fiasco. He never paused for breath as he described every aspect of his unhappy situation. Only when he finally ran down did Cliff get a chance to insert a word.

"Have you ever considered that asking a nineties woman if she'll do your laundry might be considered just a tad, uh, retro?" Cliff asked.

Todd nodded. "I was afraid of that. But it was an emergency. I swear."

Cliff lifted one eyebrow in silent query.

"It was," Todd insisted. "A grateful client gave me tickets to the Lakers game and I had to go up to L.A.—the Chicago Bulls were in town."

Cliff whistled in appreciation. Yeah, Lakers tickets

for a game of that magnitude were more precious than gold.

"And I had a big client consultation the next morning—and no clean shirts! I mean, what was I *supposed* to do?"

Cliff hardened his heart against the man-to-man appeal. "Your laundry?"

He glanced over his shoulder toward the silent patio. His masculine instinct for self-preservation told him he might find himself on shaky ground unless he got back to Mallory. He took Todd by the arm and aimed him toward the door.

"Look, Todd, it's too bad your girlfriend doesn't appreciate the necessity of going to an important basketball game—but you've got to handle your trauma by yourself. I'm busy right now." He gave a meaningful nod toward the patio.

His friend dug in his heels for a moment, then relaxed and—finally—began to cooperate in his eviction. Todd lowered his voice to a booming whisper that no doubt carried halfway down the block. "Jeez, I'm sorry, Cliff. You've got a girl here, don't you?"

Cliff nodded, still urging more progress toward the front door. "Yes. Goodbye."

"'Bye." Todd finally exited, then poked his head back in before Cliff could slam the door. "Does your babe do laundry? If so, I've got a pile at home—"

Cliff pushed Todd's head out and slammed the

door shut. What a disaster! Still, he'd managed to get rid of his buddy in only—he checked his watch—seventeen minutes, a new record. With steps that grew jauntier by the second, he walked back to the patio, only to stop short at the threshold.

Two perfectly tossed salads, glistening with dressing, sat in splendor on the table, while the cooked salmon kept warm off to one side of the grill. But it wasn't the teasing aroma of marinated fish or raspberry vinaigrette that stopped him in his tracks. It was the even more tempting sight of Mallory, curled up in a lounge chair like a contented kitten, her head nestled in one hand, her legs drawn up in a sexy curve....

And her eyes closed in deep sleep.

# 4

DISAPPOINTMENT BURNED like acid in Cliff's veins. He took one slow step onto the patio, then stopped again. Should he wake her? Or let her sleep?

*Wake her up! Wake her up! You've been waiting for this for days. It's time to get this affair going.*

But his nobler half had a different argument. *Yes, but she was so tired earlier. She even admitted she hasn't been sleeping well. It'd be cruel to wake her now that she's finally resting.*

While the debate raged within him, he softly moved to the gas grill and turned it off. He eyed the salads waiting on the patio table. Maybe he should take them inside to the refrigerator? They could be brought out again later when…if…

"Your visitor gone?" Mallory's voice, always slightly husky, now was more of a contented purr.

"You're awake?" His knees almost buckled. He'd spent hours this past week imagining the sound of her voice when she first woke, but the reality was like the velvet rasp of a kitten's tongue against his ear. Soothing. Tickling. And arousing, definitely arousing.

She smiled. "Awake and hungry," she confirmed. "Where are you taking those salads?"

"Nowhere. Not if you're ready to eat." He plunked the plates back onto the table, moved her glass of sangria to her place setting, and gave her a hand up, almost in the same motion. "I'll get the salmon."

But though the meal went down smoothly and the conversation was amiable, Cliff couldn't figure out how to make the transition from friendly chatter to ardent loving. It wasn't a problem he'd often had, he admitted silently. Usually he had no difficulty on his dates with women. But Mallory was, well, different. Why, exactly, he couldn't quite explain, even to himself. But she just was.

*You don't want to rush her. You don't want her to think you're only after her body.* Well, maybe, he admitted silently. But it wasn't as if he *didn't* want her body—as soon as possible. It was just that…hell, he didn't have any idea. Never mind that tingle of desire fizzing through his veins, never mind their no-frills agreement, he had too much respect for Mallory—and himself—to rush her into bed.

"D'you mind?"

Mallory's question jerked him out of his mental floundering. "I'm sorry. What did you say?"

"Is it okay if I do a bit of sunbathing while we're out here? My patio is impossible." She gestured at the huge eucalyptus tree that loomed over the end of the condo building. Its shadow darkened the patio of Mallory's next-door unit, though it barely affected his.

"Sure. That's fine." What male in his right mind would ever tell a gorgeous woman not to wear a skimpy bathing suit in front of him? Not he, that was for sure.

"Thanks. I wore my suit in hopes you'd say that." Before he could draw two breaths she'd slipped out of her shorts and jersey top to reveal an attractive but fairly conservative bikini. She adjusted the lounge chair flat, pulled a bottle of sunscreen from her bag, and tossed it to him. "Would you do my back?"

He forgot to draw a third breath. *You're not going to rush her. You're not going to rush her.* The mantra bongoed through his brain while he slowly uncapped the sunscreen. *This scenario could have come straight from a 1960s beach movie. She could be Annette, everyone's sweetheart. You could be…*

Nuts. That's what he could be. Certifiably, undeniably, crackers.

Sitting beside her on the lounge chair, he warmed some of the oil in his palm, then slowly smoothed it over skin as smooth as butter. The instant wriggle of contentment he felt under his hands sparked an answering swirl of arousal through him.

*You're not going to rush her. You're not going to rush her.*

Frowning, he tried to keep his mind strictly on the task at hand. He cupped his hands around those long, long legs and stroked the oil into her skin from ankles to hips. When his hands strayed into her inner thighs, he thought he heard a moan.

"Did I rub too hard?" His hands froze into position, nestled intimately between her upper thighs.

"No." Her voice was slightly muffled. "I just got a kink in my neck."

"Let me see." He moved his hands away from the far-too-dangerous territory at the top of her legs. He worked on the muscles at her shoulder and nape. "Your muscles are so tense I could bounce quarters off them."

She purred something that might have been an agreement.

He put real effort into working out her kinks, enjoying the slick blend of skin and coconut lotion. As he moved further down her back, he hesitated at the back closing of her bikini top. "Uh, do you mind?" *Dolt! What happened to your cool, man?*

But Mallory looked over her shoulder at him and gave him a slow, sleepy smile. "Go ahead."

His fingers fumbled the closure—when did he lose

every trace of finesse?—but eventually he got it open
and spread the straps wide. Now he had free range
of her body from head to toe, save only for the small
swath of material over her hips. He shifted uncomfortably to accommodate his growing arousal. His
kneading motions only reminded him of the silky
steel of her muscles and the feminine lushness of her
curves. When his hands moved around her to cup the
side swell of her breasts and refused to move away,
he'd had enough.

"Mallory. I—we—"

With the sinuous motion of a mermaid, she rolled
over. Her arms twined around his neck, tugging him
closer. "I wondered how long you'd hold out."

"You *planned* this?" His mock outrage probably
didn't have much impact when his lips nuzzled her
breast.

"Sure." Her hands busily unbuttoned his shirt.
"Well, sort of. You certainly seemed to be taking a
long time to get anywhere." She grinned. "You look
kind of cute when you're just a teensy bit embarrassed. Did you know that?"

Heat warmed the back of his neck. "I was not—
am not—embarrassed. I just didn't—don't—want to
rush you into anything."

With her fingers spearing through his hair and out-
lining the rims of his ears, he was sure she'd feel the
steam sizzling off him and recognize his claim for

the lie it was. But she just nodded. "It's okay, you know. About being embarrassed. I was, too."

"Sure you were. You were so embarrassed you told me to take off your bikini top."

It might have been a flush that tinted her cheeks pink. Or maybe it was just a trick of the sun. But her sudden stillness in his arms wasn't an illusion. "Do you want to know the truth?"

Did he? He had enough experience with women to know that truth-telling could get a man into a lot of trouble. Warily, he nodded. "I guess."

She took a deep breath and her tongue left a shiny track across sun-kissed lips. The action almost derailed Cliff's train of thought. "The truth is, while I was waiting for you to come back I started worrying about…us. And how hard it was going to be to just, well, do it. With no preliminaries or anything. And I thought that maybe you might feel the same way, so if I took things into my own hands—"

A sappy grin was spreading across his face and he couldn't do a thing to stop it. His hands moved down to cover her breasts. "Or rather, if I took things into *my* hands?"

"Yes." But the word was more gasped than articulated. "Anyway, you got the point."

His fingers plucked a crowning nipple. "And the point being?"

Her own sudden sappy grin was almost as wide as

his felt. Her hands dropped from his ears and busily explored his chest. ''The point being that you lawyers talk everything to death. You're all talk, no action.''

''No action, huh? I'll show you 'no action.''' With a mock growl, he levered her over his shoulder in a fireman's carry and toted her inside to the comfortable couch in the living room.

Within seconds, he'd stripped off her bikini bottom and his own clothes, pausing only long enough to pull a condom from his pants pocket before rolling on top of her.

She was giggling so hard and her back and legs were so slippery with sunscreen lotion that it was hard to hold on to her, but he managed to lever himself into position above her.

''What were you saying about no-action lawyers?'' His implied threat was muffled by her sizzling kiss. This woman could kiss like no woman he'd ever met before. Why hadn't he realized before that she was so incredible, fabulous, magnificent...

Words failed him as he simply reveled in the experience. Only when he grew dizzy did he break away from the kiss and nudge himself more intimately between her legs.

Her hips tilted up to accommodate his forward thrust. God, she felt wonderful! Hot and tight, like sinking into a pool of wet velvet, only softer. With a surge, he pushed into her as deep as he could manage. "God, Mallory, you're—"

From the patio a strident electronic beep demanded attention. He froze.

"—being paged." He raised his head to stare at her face. "Do you want to stop?"

"No!" She shifted her hips, and used her hands to pull him inside her even deeper. "Don't stop!"

"But—"

"Don't stop!"

But his mind never quite left that insistent chirping from the patio. As if in a bizarre race, he felt himself going faster and faster, trying to outrun that persistent call. When he finally spasmed, he realized that though he'd found his release, Mallory hadn't.

He paused only a moment to catch his breath before rolling off her. "Mallory, I'm sorry."

But she had already grabbed his shirt from the floor, wrapped it around herself, and headed for the patio. When she returned a moment later, she carried her clothes and that damned beeper. He could really learn to hate that tyrannical little device.

"I'm sorry," he said again. It was hard to apologize for something he'd really enjoyed, though he wished she'd enjoyed it as much as he had. "I know it wasn't as good for you—"

She waved his feeble excuses aside without waiting to hear them. "Don't worry about it. I've got to run. There's a big story breaking downtown. I'll call you later, okay?''

Absently, she pulled on her clothes, gave him a quick kiss, and headed for the door before he could do more than pull on his cutoffs. He trailed her, trying to sort out his jumbled feelings. But with another quick kiss and an apologetic smile, she was out the door before he could even begin to make sense of his roiling emotions.

He mooched around his condo, clearing away the remnants of their meal, and tried to make sense of his snarled emotions. He seldom spent time in introspection, but he finally collapsed with a can of beer on the couch—a couch that still exuded an intoxicating blend of coconut and Mallory—and tried to concentrate on the situation.

What the hell *did* he feel about what had happened, anyway? Relief she wasn't mad at his failure to satisfy her? Yes. Disappointment? Sure. He'd always liked cuddling after sex. Maybe a little bit of resentment that she could dismiss him so easily?

*No way!* He understood her commitment to her job. He had the same commitment to his. They'd settled that from the first. He was just…concerned, yes, that must be it. He was worried that she was off to some dangerous assignment—maybe a drug bust or the SWAT team capture of some mad serial killer?—where no one would protect her. He blithely dismissed the technicians and crew that would no doubt be beside her every step of the way, and he just as easily put aside his ignorance of the kind of story she was covering. None of that mattered. He wanted her here, with him, not off doing something dangerous.

*But she doesn't want to be here with you. At least not right this moment.*

Hmm. A good point. And why should she? So far, their attempts to start an affair with "great sex and no commitments" had achieved the "no commitments" part and even the "sex" part—but "great"? Well, for him, maybe, or at least "good." But for her? Hardly.

Fair was fair. That *had* to change.

He brooded long into the fading afternoon, mapping out a plan designed to guarantee that the next time he got Mallory Reissen alone, she was going to end up more sexually satisfied than any woman in history.

He would guarantee it.


MALLORY DROVE downtown to cover the governor's impromptu visit to San Diego, lending only half her attention to the road. The rest was firmly centered on a certain condo in La Jolla where she'd left her new lover behind.

*Lover.* Somehow, the word didn't quite describe

her relationship with Cliff. Associate? Colleague? Date? Boyfriend? She grimaced and shifted lanes to pass a car. None of those fit, either.

*Maybe after he thinks about this afternoon, he'll be your ex-lover.*

There was always that possibility. Darn it! They'd been friends ever since he'd moved into the condo next to hers. One less-than-perfect sexual encounter shouldn't change that. Sure, he knew she hadn't climaxed. Men didn't like knowing that, in her experience. They wanted to be considered the best thing in the sack since penny candy. But this afternoon, with her mind fretting over the insistent pager, her embarrassment at making the first move, even the natural awkwardness of a first time together, she simply hadn't been able to relax enough.

Suddenly a new question loomed. Did he realize that her nerves were to blame for their less-than-world-shattering lovemaking? Cliff was a really nice guy—she knew that—after all, that's why she'd proposed their affair in the first place. He was one of the good guys. He could be trusted, not just with her body, but her feelings, too. She trusted him not to expect too much, just as he trusted her not to read too much into his lovemaking.

Still, maybe he was beating up on himself for something that wasn't his fault.

Would he understand that things would probably be a lot better next time?

*Would there* be *a next time?*

She turned onto the freeway exit ramp and pondered that question. Next time, she'd make sure things went well, she promised herself. She'd make up for today's nervousness and too-quick departure. She'd be sweet, charming, and make sure he knew she didn't blame him for anything.

Yes, that was it. She'd be sweet, charming, gracious—and she'd climax so obviously that he could be in no doubt of his prowess as a lover.

She guaranteed it.

BUT SHE HADN'T counted on "next time" happening on a day that combined all the delights of Friday the thirteenth, an IRS audit, and a *really* bad hair day.

"Hi, Mallory." Cliff straightened as she approached where he leaned against his car in the condominium parking lot. He gave her a warm peck on the cheek. "I'm glad you decided you could come out and play tonight."

"It's been a tough day," she said, reluctant to move. She'd arrived home twenty minutes ago, with just enough time to change clothes before meeting him. It was "hump-day"—Wednesday—after a half week that already seemed as long as a month. The aspirin she'd gulped hadn't yet touched her throbbing head, a new perm and unusual humidity had her looking like the Bride of Frankenstein, and she'd had separate fights with both the news producer and the station makeup artist. Not to mention having an incipient case of PMS that promised to be a lulu.

Still, when Cliff had called earlier to say he was taking the entire evening off and couldn't she come with him for a late dinner, she couldn't find a way to say no. She wanted to be with him, lousy mood, lingering headache, cramping stomach and all. While exhausted disgruntlement scratched sex from her personal agenda for this particular evening, she knew she could count on Cliff for a sympathetic ear and a relaxing good time. Besides, when she'd delicately pointed out that she wasn't in the mood for a sleepover, he'd insisted that didn't matter. Still, she owed him the opportunity to back out of a date that could go nowhere.

"Are you sure you want to be around me?" she asked him. "I'm pretty grumpy when I'm tired. And this has been an incredibly hellish day. Maybe I should settle for a mug of Ovaltine and an early night."

"Oh, I'm sure," he said, opening the car door. "I intend to make up for last Sunday by whisking you away from all your troubles. In fact, I think I can promise you an evening you'll never forget."

Tempted, she wavered, then conceded with a little

sigh. Maybe by the time he brought her home she'd be unwound enough to get some sleep. She surreptitiously flicked her pager to ''off'' as she stepped into the car. She needed an uninterrupted night, and this time, by George, she was going to get it. ''You did say we were going somewhere not too dressy, didn't you?'' She gestured at her designer jeans and simple short-sleeved cotton-ramie sweater.

''You look perfect.''

''And I'll never forget this evening?'' She fastened the seat belt. ''Sounds like a lot for you to live up to.''

''Don't worry.'' He closed the door and walked around to the driver's side. ''I think I can impress you. I've been working hard and I'm in the mood to have a little fun. You game?''

Mallory nodded, leaned against the seat back and closed her eyes, not bothering to pay attention to where Cliff drove them. She wasn't sure she cared where they went. She wasn't all that hungry—the knot of tension that lodged just under her breastbone ensured she'd eat little, anyway.

The whole week had been a disaster, starting with Sunday's unsatisfactory tryst and capped by her agent's call that morning telling her the network honchos had put off her job interview for another two weeks. Lenny had even agreed with her morose assessment that it probably meant they had someone else in mind and might never even get around to talking to her. With her hopes of a huge career advancement fading, she retreated again into her dour gloom. She simply wasn't in the mood for dinner at some upscale restaurant where she'd be expected to be ''on'' all evening.

She could envision the meal already. Cliff was trying to impress her, he'd said. That probably meant a trendy restaurant where the service staff had names like Tiffany or Darryl and the noise factor was loud enough to make sure no meaningful conversation could possibly take place. The menu would feature only the most fashionable ingredients—was this month's favorite the chiles that gave her gas, the cilantro that left a nasty taste in her mouth, or the exotic fungus that reminded her of some alien lifeform? Whichever, everyone would be so busy posturing to impress those around them that no one would pay the slightest attention to anyone else.

She'd seen it all a hundred times. Resigned, Mallory mentally condemned herself to another inedible meal that cost five times as much as it should. She wondered if she had enough antacid in her medicine chest to make it through the inevitable night of heartburn.

Just once, she thought wistfully, just once I'd like to go somewhere…different.

HE TOOK HER TO a bowling alley.

When Cliff opened the door to the moderately busy lanes and escorted Mallory inside, he took a deep breath. Familiar odors of hot grease from the snack bar, sweaty rental shoes and chalk from the battered pool table in the far alcove assaulted his nostrils, bringing on a wave of bittersweet nostalgia. The hum of conversation, the clatter of pins falling, and the rumble of the pin-spotting machines strummed his ears like his favorite song from high school.

He'd spent many a pleasant hour hanging out here when he was about thirteen. While his mother flipped burgers in the snack bar, he'd become unofficial after school pinspotter for the owner, taking his pay in free games and meals instead of money.

His mother had hung on to that job for more than a year—one of her longest stints anywhere—and Cliff remembered the place with more fondness than most of the joints she'd slaved in. Besides, Bertie, the alley owner, had taken one look at Felicia Young's half-wild kid and opened his heart to him. Cliff knew that without Bertie's intervention he could well have ended up in some street gang instead of an expensive condo.

Hell, he'd even brought Rebecca Salinger, his first sweetheart in junior high, here on their first date. And snatched a kiss in the hard plastic seats of the next-

to-last lane. The distant memory of that innocent em-
brace evoked a recollection of far more heated kisses
with Mallory. This time, he vowed again silently,
she'd find satisfaction from more than his kisses.

"Let's get you some bowling shoes," he said,
guiding her to the desk. "What size do you wear?"

"Cliff, I don't think—"

"Yo, Cliff! How ya been? Been a while, hasn't
it?" Bertie said. The butterball man's gap-toothed
grin warmed Cliff like a wood fire in winter.

"Hi, Bertie. Ready to go grunioning again?" On
Cliff's last visit Bertie had closed the lanes early,
then he and Cliff had headed for the beaches of La
Jolla to watch the grunions do their spawning dance
in the moonlight.

"Maybe. Or maybe you've got better company."
Bertie gave Mallory an openly salacious wink.
"What size shoe do you take, darlin'?"

"I'm not—"

Overriding her protests, Cliff said, "Give her a
size seven, I think. And I'll take elevens."

"I'm not—"

Lowering his head so his mouth was right beside
her ear, he whispered, "Sure you are. Remember?
When I asked where you wanted to eat you told me
to pick someplace I wanted to go. Well, this is it."

She turned her head, tickling his chin with a few
stray hairs and leaving her cheek only millimeters

from his mouth. God, how he wanted to close that distance!

"You know I didn't mean—"

"Bowling? It'll do you good. Besides, it's fun, good exercise, and I want to do it." Deliberately, he closed the span between their flesh until barely a whisper separated them. "Don't worry. I won't laugh, no matter how bad you are. All you have to do is give me an adoring smile every time I make a strike."

His ploy worked. He saw her competitive spirit surge in the glare she gave him. "I see," she said ominously. Her lips parted in what probably looked like a smile to anyone watching, but which he knew bore more similarity to the snarling challenge of a lioness.

Hastily, he drew back his head. Just in case. "Good," he said and handed her the shoes, then showed her where to choose a ball.

But it was no accident that he led the way to the battered next-to-last lane hardly anyone used these days. The one directly under the fluorescent tube that for twenty years or more had flickered stubbornly between full illumination and occasional sudden darkness. The lane with the crack in the seat that made only half of it usable, forcing a comfortable squeeze if two people sat in it at the same time.

It was the perfect spot to ensure an illusion of privacy with the woman he intended to seduce.

GIVE AN ADORING SMILE? Sure she would, Mallory thought. Right after hell froze over.

"Didn't you mention food?" she said as soon as she'd dumped her purse on the appalling flamingo-pink seat. A few lanes away, balls rumbled down the hardwood floor and pins chattered in defeat. "My stomach's so hollow I may start chewing on a bowling pin."

"Never let it be said that I disappointed a lady. What do you want on your dog?"

"You're buying me a whole hot dog? What a prince."

"Well," he rubbed his chin with stone-faced glee, "it's either that or the *chiles rellenos* or bean burritos, and I can't recommend them. They give me gas."

Maybe she *wasn't* the only person in America who couldn't eat hot chiles. "All right. I'd like mustard, relish, onions, and cheese."

"Onions?"

Sternly she frowned at his devilishly quirked eyebrow. "Lots of onions," she repeated firmly.

"Okay. I guess I'll have onions, too." He sent a too-adorable-to-be-true grin her way. "They say it doesn't matter if both participants eat them."

Before she could do more than frown, he left for the snack bar.

He returned a few minutes later with a tray holding a huge pile of greasy french fries, two wrapped but equally grease-shiny hot dogs with appropriate fixings, and two large beers.

"You realize there's enough cholesterol on that plate to clog the Alaskan pipeline?" Despite her words, she reached for her share of his booty.

"C'mon. How often do you get one of Bertie's gourmet dogs? One meal won't hurt. Indulge yourself." His voice dropped to a tempting snake-in-the-garden murmur. "Sin a little."

Surprisingly, the food was good—no, it was scrumptious. If only she could have ignored the heat he radiated as effortlessly as he breathed, she might even have admitted to enjoying the meal.

She picked up a french fry and had almost popped it into her mouth when Cliff's hand stopped hers.

"Hold it a second."

Automatically she froze, her lips forming an *O* around the end of the fry. Before she could ask what the problem was, he lowered his head and sent his tongue on a steam-heated lick across the corner of her mouth and chin. Instantly her thoughts scattered and toppled like all ten pins in a strike.

He sat back to admire his accomplishment. "There. That's fine."

Though he released her hand, Mallory almost choked before she could get the bite of french fry swallowed. "What was that for?" Not that she cared why, particularly. All she really wanted was to feel his tongue stroking her skin again—and again. Her lousy mood was getting more and more slippery with every moment. Pretty soon, she'd lose her grip on it altogether.

He cranked up her body temperature another notch or two by retracing his tongue's path with a gentle finger. "You had a smear of mustard right here."

"You ever heard of napkins, Young?"

"Napkins? Gee, now there's a concept. I never thought of them." His smile would definitely have tempted Eve to chop down the Tree of Knowledge. "Besides, they're no fun."

"Is that what we're here for? Fun?" Even to herself her words sounded wistful.

"You bet. Didn't I promise you a night you'd never forget?"

Mallory glanced around the slightly seedy bowling alley and suddenly saw the humor in the situation. Her lips curved upward in a rueful smile that broke through her grump, melting it and washing it away. She finished her beer with a long swallow. "I think you've succeeded. I can honestly say that none of my dates has ever—" the beer she swallowed too hastily made her hiccup "—treated me to a lively evening at a bowling alley."

"That's because they lacked imagination. I, on the other hand, have *plenty* of creativity. Not to mention inspiration." Cliff finished his hot dog and took a final gulp of beer before looking at her expectantly. "You ready to let me trounce you bowling?"

"Look, Cliff, I really don't want—"

"That's what you said about your hot dog, and you liked it, didn't you?"

"Yes, but—"

"So let's have some fun."

"I told you…" Darn it all, why couldn't she just enjoy these moments with him? Her problems at work and with the will-o'-the-wisp network career opportunity would still be there tomorrow. Even her headache had temporarily been beaten into submission by the aspirin and her stomach was practically purring in contentment after the deliciously unhealthy meal. Why not seize this evening and wring every bit of pleasure she could from it?

With a sigh, she stood and picked up her ball. "Okay. We'll bowl."

"Great!"

She headed for the proper position and gave him her most challenging look. "But I want you to know I intend to beat the socks off you—and *I'm* keeping score."

Just as she stepped forward to roll a practice ball down the lane, she was thrown off stride by his low-voiced Bogie drawl. "Sweetheart, socks are the least of it. You can get anything you want off me—all you have to do is ask."

When her ball glided ignominiously straight into the gutter, she glared at him. "That wasn't fair! You broke my concentration."

"All's fair. Isn't that what they say?"

Darn it. There was that devilish-choirboy grin again. If he ever figured out she'd forgive him anything for that smile, she'd be dead meat. So he thought all was fair, did he? Well, he didn't know who he was daring with that comment. All was fair in love—and war. She barely restrained the impulse to do her best Groucho Marx imitation and assert, "Of course you know this means war."

Instead, she deliberately waited until he was preparing to bowl his own practice round. In the middle of his first stride she said in a butter-wouldn't-melt voice, "Don't you think that'll be a bit embarrassing with all these people around? I mean—strip bowling?"

He didn't even bother to watch his ball skitter sideways into the gutter. He loomed over her with eyes glittering promises. "Strip bowling?"

"Wasn't that what you were proposing?" she asked innocently. "Sure sounded like it to me."

After a moment studying her he asked, "What happened to that life-is-real-life-is-earnest lady I walked in here with?"

She smiled. "I found Ernest—and strangled him."

He tugged her out of her seat and into his arms as he roared with laughter. "You constantly surprise me."

"Good. So no strip bowling, huh?"

"Oh, no." Satisfaction dripped from his voice. "I'd *never* let a dare like that pass."

She looked around the alley. While it wasn't crowded—no one was closer than five lanes away—the place certainly wasn't private enough for, well, stripping. "But all these people—we'll get arrested!"

"No, we won't. Not if we do it my way."

"Your way?" Her mental alarms shrieked in warning. "What's your way?" Was she really contemplating agreeing to…?

He whispered instructions into her ear, sending tropical shivers down her spine. "We'll do it with our imaginations. With each ball, you get to describe what garment you'll remove from me if you win that frame—and what will be revealed once you remove it."

Her throat tightened into a thick clot of—nerves? *No, you dummy, it's excitement!* "Describe?" she managed to utter.

"In detail. The sound of the garment rustling. How it feels in your hands. Everything you'd experience if you removed it from me yourself. I'm talking color. Texture. Scent. Taste." His lips captured the lobe of her ear. "*Especially* taste."

Her eyelids drifted downward as rivulets of sensation rushed from her earlobe to the core of her body. It was as if his lips had found her heartstrings and plucked them deliberately. Did she dare agree to his outrageous proposal? Yet did she have the willpower to refuse?

Gathering her strength of mind, she pulled her head—and vulnerable ears—away from his mouth. "What do I get if I win?"

"What do you want?"

*You! You! You!* Her senses screamed their response. But her mind answered for her with the thing she least wanted to win yet knew she most needed after her exhausting workweek. "An early night—alone?"

Disappointment dimmed his gaze, but he nodded acceptance of her request.

"And what will you get if you win?" she asked.

Darn it. That impish choirboy was back. "Why, Mallory," he promised, "*when* I win, I get to go home and do it all over again—in person."

# 5

SHE SHOULD HAVE WON.

She would have won—if Cliff hadn't cheated. By the tenth frame, she'd managed to acquit herself pretty well. Whether through her descriptive talents or her skill at ignoring his, she'd brought her score to within one pin of Cliff's. He'd already bowled his last ball, ending with what he called a "humiliating" ninety-six score.

"It's the worst I've bowled since I was in fifth grade," he complained. "You're lethal, you know that?"

She smugly refused to admit that her current score of ninety-five was the highest she'd ever bowled in her life. By luck or the intervention of some guardian angel, she'd actually made a tenth-frame spare, knocking down all ten pins in two attempts. It was only her fourth spare of the game, and she had no idea how she'd accomplished it.

Of course, it hadn't been easy. Not when she'd mentally and verbally stripped Cliff of every article of clothing, leaving him dressed only in a pair of tight white undershorts that molded lovingly to his very masculine form. Ten frames: Two shoes. Two socks. A belt. Pants. A watch. A shirt. A T-shirt. The class ring on his finger. Despite their hurried intimacy on Sunday, she simply hadn't the courage to remove—even in imagination—that final, soft cotton covering. Or to let herself describe the delights hidden beneath it.

Her scruples certainly hadn't fazed him. He'd started with her sweater, then her bra. With each following frame, he'd returned to a detailed description of how her breasts swayed and bounced and tasted as he one by one removed her knee-high stockings, shoes, belt, and slacks.

"You have some fetish about breasts, Young?" she'd finally demanded after missing an easy spare because of his eager description of how her nipples tasted.

"Never before," he said, as if seriously considering the matter. "But I think I'm developing one about yours. Did I mention how perfectly they nestle in my palm?"

She threw up her hands and gave up chastising him.

In the ninth frame, she thought she'd faint when he deliberately explained how he would unhook her left earring and exactly where he would tuck it.

Could she hold it in her navel while she rolled the ball? The image left her breathless, and she plonked the ball awkwardly onto the lane.

It knocked over nine pins.

In the tenth frame, he described exactly how he'd rub her breasts against his own bare chest while he used his tongue to undo her right earring. His hands, he said, would be busy rubbing her hips tightly against those straining undershorts. Her mouth would be all over his chest, teasing and licking his nipples while he tugged her ear.

She was a nervous wreck, but converted a difficult seven-ten split into a impossible spare.

But that final-frame spare not only brought her to within a pin of his final score; it also gave her an extra ball to roll. If she knocked down more than one pin, she'd win the game. And it had been five or six frames since her last gutter ball.

"I hope you realize that it's all over for you, Young," she taunted as she took her position. "I'm going to beat you pretty handily."

"Does this mean you're not going to jump my bones tonight and insist on doing all those incredibly delightful things you've been describing to me? Even though I've got you naked?"

"I'm not naked!"

"Not yet," he promised. "But you've got another

ball to roll, and as far as I can see, there's only one more thing for me to remove.''

Unless he meant her nail polish, he could only be talking about her panties. A hot flush bubbled up her neck at the thought of him actually... No! She had to get her mind back on her bowling. If she didn't, she'd dump this ball in the gutter and lose. And then *he'd...*

Her eyes glazed over as she thought about that possibility. But Cliff's triumphant chuckle broke through her contemplation.

''You want to lose to me, don't you? You want me to put my fingers inside those pale pink panties—''

''They're white!'' she blurted before she could stop herself.

''Sorry. I've been picturing them as pale pink, almost the color of your skin. But white is good too. There's a shadow in the front that hints of the curls I'll find when I use my finger—no, my tongue—to ease the elastic down just a bit.'' He shook his head. ''No, that's not how I'll do it. I'll come up behind you and press you back against me. You'll feel how hard I am against your hips. I want in, and you know it. I want in *bad.*''

His voice was husky, soft, barely intelligible. Her back was to him, so he couldn't see the hard points of her breasts revealing how he aroused her. He couldn't know for sure that he was melting her to jelly with his words.

"I'll take my hand and slip it in the front of your panties, so I can play with the curls there. I'll tug them and caress them carefully. Then I'll tip my head over your shoulder so I can look down and see my fingers when they delve lower. Lower. Aaah, you're wet. You want me too, don't you? You shift your legs just far enough apart to make room for my hand. You're ready, aren't you?"

Frozen, she couldn't think what to do, couldn't remember to breathe, couldn't remember why her right arm felt so heavy. Closing her eyes was another mistake. His seductive voice grabbed every iota of her concentration.

"Your hips are straining against me, begging for me to finish it. You're gasping for breath, and your heart is beating so hard you think you're going to faint. I can feel it under my hand. I'm cupping your breast, pulling gently on your nipple."

Desperately, she found the strength to turn her head to look at him. Her vision was fogged but she saw him rise slowly and approach her.

"Need some help, Mallory?"

"Help?" *I need you. I need you to do all those things you've told me about.*

"Help rolling your ball, I mean. You've got one more chance to catch up with me."

He stood on the floor of the seating area, a step below the hardwood ramp where she stood. His eyes were almost level with hers. "Help?" It seemed the only word she could utter. With the exotic images he'd evoked scrolling before her blurred vision, she wasn't quite sure if it was a question or a plea.

He stepped up behind her, passed his left hand around her waist and used his right to guide her right arm. No wonder it felt so heavy. She had a twelve-pound bowling ball stuck at the end of it.

That's right. She was *bowling*.

"If you make a gutter ball," he whispered against her ear, "you'll lose and I'll take you home and do all those things I told you about."

"All—" Her tongue was so thick, she could barely squeeze out the syllable.

His tongue nuzzled her ear. "Uh-huh. *All*. And we haven't even gotten to the part where I take those very sexy, very white panties off you. All you have to do is roll the ball down the gutter and you get exactly what you want from me."

Deliberately, his hand drifted lower, across her abdomen, whispering across the juncture of her thighs, to hover over the place he'd been describing so erotically moments before. Hot wetness flooded through her and she melted back against him. Sure enough, his thick arousal pressed against her hips.

"Remember how I told you I'd do it? My fingers

touching you, my hand holding your breast. Remember?''

Automatically she took a step forward, but he followed with a step of his own.

''All you have to do is roll the ball down the gutter.''

Would that seductive voice never stop? What did he want of her, anyway?

''Just drop the ball down the gutter and I'll take those panties off you for real. I'll spend the night proving how good we can be together. My imagination's been running wild since Sunday, you know. We didn't get the chance to really explore our relationship. Just drop the ball in the gutter and we'll both discover the possibilities. C'mon, Mallory, all you have to do is drop the ball.''

Her mind bowed to the command in his voice. Her fingers relaxed and the ball dropped.

Into the middle of the lane.

Once she'd released the ball, she stepped away from his arms. A measure of sanity returned.

''You cheated!'' she said.

He took a deep breath, straightened slowly and walked stiff-legged back to the scoring area. It hadn't been a total put-on, she realized. The front of his pants tented outward noticeably.

''I never cheat. I don't have to.''

Her composure was seeping back. ''What do you

call putting your hands all over me while I'm trying to roll my ball?''

Humor glinted in his eyes. ''Copping a feel?''

''And trying to persuade me to throw the game by rolling a gutter ball?''

''Good strategy?''

She suddenly realized she hadn't bothered to see how her last ball had done. She swiveled back to face the pins.

It was still staggering down the lane, moving at a tortoise-slow pace. At that barely moving speed, the variations in the lane's planking gave its trajectory a definite side-to-side wobble.

''What do you want to bet it never makes it to the pins? I think I just won.'' Cliff eyed her up and down. ''I can't wait to collect my winnings.''

Steadily, the ball wavered on, slowing down with each revolution. ''C'mon, ball. Knock something over. Even a few pins will do.'' Her fists clenched, she pushed her hip forward to urge the ball on. At least it was staying in the middle of the lane, so if it made it to the pins it would almost certainly knock a few over.

''It'll never make it that far. Trust me. You lost.''

''It'll get there. I know it will.'' The ball barely inched forward, finally approaching the perfect spot for a strike, the pocket between the foremost one-pin and the three-pin just behind and to one side. "Go, baby, go! Knock 'em all down!"

But the ball wheezed to a weary halt, right beside the one-pin, giving it a nudge but not knocking down anything. The pin teetered a bit, and Mallory held her breath. Would it fall?

"The rule says if the ball doesn't make it to the pins, it counts as a gutter ball," Cliff intoned with satisfaction. "You lost."

"No! Look!" With regal slowness, the teetering one-pin finally gave up and toppled to the side, completely missing all the other pins. "I knocked one down!"

She'd tied Cliff with a score of ninety-six.

But she should have won.

MALLORY'S SMILE from her Wednesday-evening bowling adventure lingered for nearly a week. It survived crises at the station, an irritating taping session for promo shots for the upcoming May sweeps campaign, and another dead-of-night phone call from her mother. It even outlasted another network delay in interviewing her for that plum prime-time slot. The promised meeting was now nearly a month away. *If,* that was, they didn't hire someone else without even talking to Mallory.

But her satisfied smile couldn't survive a week of utter neglect from Cliff.

In her spare moments, Mallory went over every detail of that memorable evening—a process that usually resulted in an unplanned cold shower. No doubt about it, Cliff was going to be an unusually creative lover. She would never have dreamed that bowling—*bowling!*—could be so…inspiring. Even though her physical exhaustion insisted that the evening end in separate bedrooms, the memory of Cliff's seductive whispers generated a sensation that in olden times would have been called "palpitations."

Yes, despite their initial misfires, sex with Cliff would be the best she'd ever had, she was sure. A man as innately sensual and intense as he was couldn't be anything except superb in bed—once she managed to get him there. You had to expect these little awkwardnesses when starting a new relationship, she told herself firmly. Nobody's fault, really. That was just life. All she had to do was hang in there until her schedule finally meshed with Cliff's to give them some uninterrupted free time.

So why did she feel so…well, neglected?

She understood that he was working long, hard hours. For Pete's sake, she did the same. So what was wrong with her? Why couldn't she just enjoy what she had without trying to scrape up trouble where there wasn't any—or shouldn't be any?

Nevertheless, when her phone rang at nine o'clock one evening, she leaped for the receiver. "Hi!" she said, sure it *had* to be Cliff calling to tell her to come right over and "get naked."

"Darling! I'm so sorry to call you this late." Her mother's breathless, perpetually-confused-about-life's-details voice greeted her.

"Hello, Mother." *Why wasn't it Cliff calling?* "Don't worry about the time. It's only nine o'clock."

"Nine? But I thought—it's nearly midnight here, and I know you're three hours different, but I just had to get this settled..."

"Never mind, Mother. Was there something wrong?"

"No. Well, yes, dear. In a way. You remember I told you I was coming out to Stanford this spring? Well, it's settled—or rather, I changed my itinerary again. I'll be out there next week. I'd really like to do that lunch we talked about."

Lunch with her mother. Now there was a treat. "I don't know, Mother. It's pretty hard for me to get away during the week—especially when it's so far away. It'll take all day to shuttle up to the Bay Area, have lunch, then take a shuttle back."

"Oh, my dear, didn't I say? It would have to be on a Saturday. I'll be working closely with Peter Jonassen, you know. Such a wonderful researcher. What he found on those digs in Ur...well! Anyway, I'll be tied up until the weekend for sure. Let me see, that would be Saturday, the fourteenth. Is that all right?''

''Well...'' Mallory had hoped to convince Cliff to go away with her on that particular weekend. But realistically, he'd probably spend the day working anyway. Why not make her mother happy and go to lunch with her? At the very least, it would be something to do that would keep her mind off Cliff. For a while.

''Sure, Mother. I'll be there. Just tell me where you're staying and I'll rent a car and pick you up.'' Mallory knew her mother had a phobia about driving in an unfamiliar town.

As she scribbled down the address her mother rattled off, Mallory's eyebrow rose. ''You're staying with Dr. Jonassen? At his house?''

''Oh, yes, dear,'' her mother practically chirped. ''He's such a nice man. So accommodating. When he found out that your father wouldn't be coming with me, he insisted I stay with him. I'll be much more comfortable there than in some motel, he said, and it'll be easy for him to give me rides wherever I need to go. Isn't that sweet of him?''

Sweet. Mallory rolled her eyes. ''Sure, Mother. I'll see you then on the fourteenth.'' But as she hung up, her pen tapped the paper thoughtfully. Her father was in Europe again, and her mother was flying cross-country to work with a male professor—and staying in the man's house, to boot. Surely her mother wouldn't...couldn't...

No. Her parents' marriage, strange and unsatisfying as it seemed to her, worked well for them. She was just imagining things. This Dr. Jonassen was probably in his late seventies, married, and had seven grandkids.

Never mind that, *why didn't Cliff call?*

AFTER TWO MORE DAYS of waiting fruitlessly, Mallory took advantage of a break at work and picked up her office phone. The door was tightly closed and she had perhaps ten minutes before someone would come knocking and demand her presence. With fingers that trembled unaccountably, she pressed the sequence of digits for Cliff's work phone.

"Young here."

God, it felt so good to hear his voice! "Hi, Cliff. It's me, Mallory." *Please don't let him say, "Mallory who?"*

"Mallory! Damn, but it's good to hear from you! I'm up to my eyeballs in work and this is the first good thing that's happened to me all day."

A sigh of relief trembled through her. "I'm sorry things are so tied up there. Is there anything wrong?"

She heard his chair creak and she imagined him leaning back and putting his feet on something—a wastebasket? A drawer from his desk? "Nah. Just too much work to do in too little time. Uh, say, Mallory…''

He was going to apologize for not calling her. She could hear it in his voice. But the rules they'd established at the beginning of their relationship were suddenly emblazoned in huge Day-Glo orange letters before her eyes. He'd *hate* apologizing for tending to his career ambitions.

Before he could do so, she interrupted. ''I'm sorry I've been so busy lately,'' she lied. ''But it's been really hectic here at work. I guess it's a good thing you understand about that.''

''No problem,'' he admitted. Mallory fancied she heard a note of relief in his voice. ''I've been swamped, too.''

''Well, I just had a really terrific idea.''

''Terrific, huh? Does it include bowling?''

She laughed. ''Not this time. It's going to take me a while to recover from our last excursion.''

''Darn. Bowling with you is really, um, interesting. Did I tell you how much I enjoyed last Wednesday night?''

She hesitated. ''Even though we didn't, uh…''

''Even though,'' he said solemnly. ''I just wanted to be with you. Maybe teach you a few bowling tricks of the trade. So to speak.''

*Some tricks!* Hot blood warmed her cheeks, but she disciplined her voice to a more serious note.

"Um, thanks. What I really called about is this. I've been working so hard lately, and I know you have too, that we've hardly had time to, well, be together. If you know what I mean."

His soft chuckle rippled down her spine. "Yeah, I know. And I'm not real happy about that either, as a matter of fact."

"Well, I happen to have been given a certificate for a free stay at the new five-star Maison Shores Resort. Some kind of promotional offer to the media. And I thought if we could get away from it all, even for a night, it might be, um, fun."

"Fun." He echoed the word in a way that sent another thrill down her back. "Better-than-bowling fun? Or did you have something else in mind?"

"*Definitely* better-than-bowling fun. The certificate is for one of their honeymoon cottages." Mallory tried but couldn't keep the hopeful expectation out of her voice.

"Hmm. Let me get my calendar." A rustle of papers sounded in her ear. "How about this weekend?"

Mallory pulled her own organizer toward her. "I can't this weekend. I'm scheduled to do a shoot up in Temecula. Somebody claims they found some Bigfoot footprints in one of the wineries there, and that always gets good airplay. Can we pick a weekday?"

"Well," Cliff suggested, "how about next Thursday? I don't have to be in the office until noon Friday, so we could sleep in.''

"No. Thursday's out. I'm covering the nine o'clock news for the cable news channel that night. How about Tuesday?''

"No way. I've got dinner with the defense team on the Bartlett trial. What about next weekend?''

This was getting ridiculous. "I can't,'' Mallory said. "I've promised to go up to the Bay Area for lunch with my mother on Saturday.''

"Just Saturday?''

"Uh-huh.'' A thought struck her. "You know, I'm only going up and back on Saturday. It'll be late when I get back, but...how about next Sunday? We could go straight from there to work Monday morning.''

A tappity-tap in her ear told her that he was flicking his pen against something hard while thinking about her suggestion. "You know, that might work out fine. I really ought to work on Saturday, anyway. Sunday the fifteenth it is.''

Mallory wrote the date in pen in her calendar. This was one event she refused to alter. "I'll go ahead and confirm the reservations,'' she said, but then didn't quite know what else to say. *Can we get together tonight, too?* Too pushy. *I miss you in bed.* Too needy. *How about a simple, "I miss you"?*

That one took more courage than she had.

Silence thundered on the phone lines. Finally, Cliff said, "I guess I'd better get back to work."

"Yeah. Me, too." But she didn't hang up. "Cliff?"

"Yes?"

"Is it always going to be like this between us? Having to schedule things weeks in advance just to see each other's face?"

She'd blurted out the question before she had time to consider how he might react—or even how she would react. She had the convenient affair she'd wanted—didn't she? No strings to mess up her work schedule. No recriminations. No ugly scenes.

*But not much sex, either.*

"I don't know, Mallory. I guess we have other priorities right now than each other."

"Of course. You're right. I'm just…tired."

"You'll call me, though, if you ever need me, won't you? For anything?"

*Sure. And the next time you have a free moment— say, sometime next October—I'm sure you'll do your best to help.* The bitter upwelling took Mallory by surprise. But she stifled the comment before it could spill out. "No problem, Cliff. You too. If you need anything, I mean."

"Yeah. Me too." After the briefest of pauses, Cliff said a simple goodbye and hung up the phone.

But as Mallory slowly lowered the receiver, she

stared bitterly at her jam-packed calendar. How could this affair possibly be considered a convenience when simply finding a mutually agreeable time and place to get together took a logistics specialist?

Still, next Sunday would clear things up between them. She and Cliff would have a wonderful time and they'd both end up feeling better. He hadn't been disappointed in her, nor was he angry or upset. He was simply being himself—an overworked, driven man struggling to rise to the top of his chosen career. His ambition sometimes meant that personal issues and relationships occasionally fell by the wayside in life—for a time, anyway.

But it was just temporary. It didn't mean he didn't care about her or their relationship. It merely meant he was exactly the man she thought he was.

He was, in fact, just like her.

# 6

A WEEK LATER Cliff smashed the ball against the back wall of the handball court and stepped back so Todd could take a swipe. Though his stroke was as hard as ever, Cliff's heart and soul weren't in the regular Friday afternoon game.

He needed a heart-to-heart with his best friend.

Unfortunately, Todd, perhaps scenting a rare victory, was concentrating more on returning Cliff's killer serves than responding to Cliff's tentative overtures.

"Didja see that? What a great save! I'm finally gonna win one from you, good buddy."

"Sure you will." Cliff sent the ball on another ricochet around the court. "Todd, I wanted to ask you something."

"Pleading for mercy already?" Todd smashed the ball back, but it took an unfortunate bounce off the corner, deadening its flight. "Damn."

Easily, Cliff captured the ball and held on to it.

He'd never get Todd's attention as long as they were playing. "You win," he declared.

"What? What's going on?"

"I'm calling it quits. You win. I lose."

"But, but—"

"Look, Todd, I need to talk to you, okay?"

"Well, sure. But you didn't need to concede the game just to talk."

"Yes, I did," Cliff said grimly. "This is serious."

With a penetrating glance, Todd shut up. They gathered their equipment bags and let themselves out of the court, heading for the locker room.

"What's up, Cliff?" Todd finally asked as they started to undress for the shower.

Now that he had his friend's attention, Cliff hardly knew where to begin. There were some issues he needed to discuss, but client confidentiality was also a problem. He couldn't give even his best buddy any details of the dilemma he faced.

"Is it about that babe you had over at your place a couple of Sundays ago?" Todd asked. "Listen, I'm sorry I interrupted."

"Don't worry. You weren't a problem." No, the only problem with Mallory was himself. Though he'd walked around all week in a near-continual state of frustration, he was starting to worry seriously. He'd hardly been at his finest while racing her pager, and though she'd apparently had a great time bowling, she'd still sent him to his own bed—alone.

*You're obsessing about her—and you have other issues to deal with! Cut it out!* Resolutely, he started undressing while he focused on his other big problem, the one that had led him to seek Todd's advice.

Todd shoved his handball shorts and T-shirt into his gym bag and grabbed a towel. "Sure sounds like *something's* wrong, buddy. What is it?"

Naked except for the towel wrapped around his waist, Cliff sank onto the bench in front of his locker. "I'm in a situation at work," he said slowly. "I can't be too specific."

"Yeah. Client confidentiality." Todd sat down too. "So what can you tell me?"

Cliff rubbed his hand along his jaw. "The bottom-line issue is that I don't really approve of how one of our cases is being handled."

Actually, he totally disagreed with the defense team's plan. Because so much evidence strongly indicated their client's guilt, the attorneys had come up with a strategy that attacked the personal life of the police detective investigating the case. If they could change the focus of the jury's attention to the policeman's situation instead of the murder case itself, they believed their client might be acquitted.

"One of your cases?" Todd asked.

"Well...not exactly. One of the firm's cases."

Cliff still hoped to be assigned to the Bartlett defense team, but despite his hard work supporting the partners who were the primary attorneys, so far he hadn't officially been named an associate on the case. And though he was uneasy with the defense plans, the case would certainly be a career-maker.

Todd grinned and stood. "If it's not your client, then it's not your problem."

"Yes, but—"

"No buts about it, buddy. I take it that one of the senior partners is running the case?"

"Yes."

"Then all the more reason for you to keep out of it. Never bite the hand that hands out promotions— and partnerships."

Dammit. Cliff knew his friend was right. Sheer common sense told him not to argue with the boss when trying to get that same boss to approve him for a plum position—and eventually name him to a partnership.

Still…he grabbed an antacid from his bag and slowly followed Todd toward the showers. The chalky taste of the tablet concentrated his attention while he pondered what to do. Sunday was only two days away. He would see Mallory then. Maybe she'd have some words of wisdom on this issue. At the very least, getting away with her—even for a day— seemed like a really good idea.

His stomach churning despite the tablet, he showered and dressed, then reluctantly walked from the athletic club back to his office three blocks away. Piles of work awaited him, not to mention another gut-twisting Bartlett strategy meeting. Absently, he pulled out another antacid tablet and chewed it in a preemptive move. His steps dragged, and he realized he was counting the hours until he could escape his no-win situation and be alone with Mallory.

MALLORY SAT ACROSS the damask-draped restaurant table from her fluttery mother and wondered why she'd bothered to fly half the length of the state to meet her. It was always difficult to break through her mother's "the Eminent Dr. Adelaide Reissen" persona to reach the woman underneath, and it was generally such a futile effort, most of the time Mallory didn't bother trying.

So far, the luncheon conversation had centered around her mother's anthropological digs, departmental politics in the small but prestigious New England university where her mother worked, and the truly excellent attributes of Peter Jonassen.

Mallory's initial curiosity about her mother's possible relationship with Professor Jonassen had yielded to an odd combination of certainty that Adelaide indeed was having an affair, and a dispassionate, who-cares attitude that startled her more than any insight into her mother's possible love life. Granted, she was hardly her mother's confidante, and her parent's relationship—or lack of one—was none of her business at this stage in her life. But shouldn't she feel, well, *something?*

She was so engrossed in puzzlement over her own cold-blooded view of the situation that she almost missed Adelaide's abrupt change of subject.

"—but I've been boring you, haven't I, dear? Besides, I'm sure you agree with me about the utter *egotism* of grad students these days. Things were different when I was younger, let me tell you."

Mallory smiled and nodded, the only reaction Adelaide needed. In common with many brilliant people, her mother had little use for opinions differing from her own.

"…I wanted to tell you why I asked to meet you, dear. Of course, it's always a pleasure to lunch with you, but I'm so *busy* these days that… Anyway, I was talking with your father a few weeks ago—did I tell you that his concerts are getting absolutely *brilliant* reviews? Well, he called me from Prague—or was it Belgrade? These international telephone connections are so bad, you know.…"

Mallory smiled, nodded, and crumbled another bite of roll. A sip of the crisp Chardonnay helped her focus on her mother's digressions. Adelaide would get to the point eventually.

Mallory's attention drifted again to the subject of her mother's probable affair. Was this the first one? No, surely not. It couldn't be. She was far too casual about it. How had Mallory lived nearly twenty-eight years and not realized that her parents' marriage was so flawed? Or had she subconsciously known all along?

The effort of swallowing a bitter laugh burned her throat. That question was easily answered: What with all those nannies and boarding schools, Mallory had seen so little of her parents while growing up that they could have had regular Tuesday-night orgies and she wouldn't have known anything about it.

One thing was certain, though. Mallory knew that her children, if she ever had any, would be raised by her and not some nanny. And she'd make sure they had a daddy who'd be there for them. Mallory would rather have no family at all than subject her children to the chilly upbringing that she'd experienced.

Was that why she was so unwilling to focus on anything except her career? The thought frightened her. Maybe her career-is-all attitude arose because she was afraid any attempt to combine work and family would leave her family floundering as she had.

Looking back, the only truly family time she could remember from her childhood were the precious weeks of summer vacation visiting her—

"—Grandmother Lawrence, dear. You do remember my telling you about it, I hope?"

Startled by the mention of the very person she'd been thinking of, Mallory blinked, then said, "I'm sorry, Mother. I was woolgathering. What did you say?"

Fingers stained brown from the sun tapped irritably on the table. "I said that when your father called a few weeks ago, he reminded me about your legacy from Grandmother Lawrence. I told you about it, I'm sure."

"Legacy? From Gramma?"

"Yes. When she died you were still a child, of course, so it's been in trust for quite some time. Till your majority of course, and then... It's not much, I'm afraid. At least not financially."

Mallory thought about that for at least fifteen seconds. "Mother, I'm twenty-eight. Shouldn't I have been told about this before now?" She strove to keep her voice patient and low.

But her mother shrugged. "Really, Mallory, it's been well taken care of. Your father and I have made good arrangements. We've both been so busy, you know, and we never quite got around to telling you. It's only that huge old house up in Sunfield. When your grandmother died, we hired a cleaning service to pack up all her things and store them for you, and a management company to rent the place out. They kept good tenants, at least until now.'' She leaned forward and dropped her voice to state-secret levels. ''Now that the senior man of the management firm has retired, I'm afraid the company has really gone downhill.''

''But...''

Her mother steamrolled over her protest. ''The trust was supposed to last until you were of an age to look after it yourself. Well, your father received some notice from the property manager recently, and when we discussed it, we realized that we really should simply turn things over to you and let you handle it. It's been quite a drain on our time all these years, you know.''

Mallory's mouth opened and closed twice. She'd never realized her grandmother had left her property. The house—her house!—was in Sunfield, a little town in the foothills of the Sierras, deep in the heart of California's Gold Country. Slowly, she forced her attention back to her mother's words. But while she accepted a folder of papers and a key ring from her mother, one thought kept drumming through her brain. She owned her grandmother's house! The one place in the world where she had been happy and contented. She *owned* it!

Only when she was waiting for her flight back to San Diego to board did she remember that though she might own a house in the Sierras, her career was likely to whisk her permanently to New York City.

ALL THROUGH THE short drive up the coast to the posh resort on Sunday evening, Cliff wondered how he could ever-so-casually raise the subject of his problems at work. He glanced quickly at Mallory, then returned his gaze to the heavy end-of-weekend traffic. Last-minute delays had ruined their intended midday departure.

"How was your visit with your mother?" *Well, that really got the conversation moving in the direction you wanted, didn't it?* If he hadn't been driving, he'd have slapped his palm against his forehead in frustration.

But Mallory had taken his tentative question as a signal to talk about her trip. She swiveled in her seat, making the silky skirt of her sundress swirl above her knees. "Fine. You know, it was the oddest thing. I couldn't figure out why my mother had been so insistent that I meet her."

Only half listening to her, he nodded. How could he bring up the subject he really wanted to discuss?

*Mallory, I've got a problem at work.* Nope. Might destroy her faith in him as a go-getting success story.

*Got any advice for an up-and-coming attorney?* Ditto.

*Mallory, can we talk?* No way! Too gossip-show.

In fact, every single opening line he came up with seemed to show him in a less than wonderful light. Surely any really competent guy should be able to handle a minor conflict with his boss—right? The acid taste in his mouth burned downward into his stomach. Automatically, he reached for the now ever-present roll of antacid tablets.

Did having an affair of convenience include listening to each other's professional sob stories? Regretfully, he shook his head slightly. Maybe not. Maybe sharing too much with her would only drive her further away. On the other hand, some women loved to think themselves important to a man. Was she one of them? He glanced speculatively at her and gave another tentative nod. She might be one of them....

"Was that a yes or a no?" Mallory's amused tone jerked him out of his reverie.

"What?" Had she asked one of those sneaky *relationship* questions? Hell's bells. What had he missed? He'd learned long ago that the only recourse a man had in such a situation was to apologize quickly—even if he wasn't sure for what. "I'm sorry, Mallory. I was thinking about something else. What did you ask me?"

She patted him on the knee and he stifled a relieved sigh. He'd guessed right. Dealing with women could be tricky, all right.

"You're not listening to me, are you?"

*Oh, no. The worst possible accusation!* "Of course I am! I've heard every word." What had she said? Beginning to panic, he reran his mental tape of her conversation. "You said something about the reason your mother asked you to meet her for lunch."

"That's right. You see…"

His mind drifted off as she explained about some small legacy her grandmother had left her. Making sure he responded often enough to keep her talking, he retreated again. He really wanted to talk about the situation at work—a lot. He'd love to get her take on what he should do. But the could-he, should-he, would-he doubts were eating at his confidence.

By the time they'd checked into the resort and had been shown to a truly luxurious private cottage, those doubts had grown so large they could have stomped Godzilla into the ground. He shifted his shoulders uncomfortably, trying to ease the knot of muscles that had taken up permanent residence between his shoulder blades. It seemed so tight he doubted a two-week stay in the resort's massage room could loosen it. And that didn't even include the pounding headache that threatened to redefine the word *torture* for him. All symptoms of tension, he knew.

Somewhere on that drive north, he'd given up discussing his work dilemma with Mallory, he realized. Now, all he wanted to do was hide his unusual lack of decisiveness from her. He simply couldn't bring himself to admit his self-doubts and failings to a woman he so deeply admired for her own career skills.

Besides, they hadn't planned this excursion as a way for him to dump his problems on her. No, he was going to prove to her that he could be the sensitive, caring lover she deserved. After their first romantic fiasco and their near miss with the bowling, he had a reputation to live up to—if only one in his own mind.

It had been days since he'd so much as caught a glimpse of her coming and going, and it was more than time they got their long-anticipated affair off the ground. Hadn't he promised to give her the sexual satisfaction she wanted? Ruefully he admitted that if he was feeling deprived, she must be feeling downright neglected.

At the thought, his head throbbed harder and his stomach churned even more. Automatically, he reached for another antacid pill, only to find the roll empty.

''They've done a beautiful job with these cottages, haven't they?'' Mallory was still inspecting their accommodations. ''Have you noticed the bathroom? It's got a huge Jacuzzi in it.''

''That's good.''

''I thought I'd put in a wake-up call for tomorrow

morning. I've got to be at the station early. Is six-thirty all right with you?''

"Sure. Uh, Mallory? Wasn't there a small shop by the registration desk?''

"Yes.'' Her brows arched in surprise. "Why?''

"I forgot something and I don't want to have to run out to a drugstore.''

She smiled. "Don't worry.'' She dug into her small bag, bringing out an unopened box of condoms. An extra-large box, he noticed. "I brought them. I knew you've been very busy this week and thought you might forget.''

Cliff sucked in a deep breath. The pressure building inside him cranked up another notch. "That's good. But I ran out of antacids and my stomach is bothering me.''

"Oh.'' Her brow pleated in concern. "You're having a lot of stomach problems, aren't you? Have you had your doctor check for an ulcer?''

He shook his head and backed toward the door. "I'm okay. But work is pretty stressful right now. It sometimes interferes with my digestion. Once this case is over, I'll be fine.''

"If you say so,'' she said doubtfully.

But as Cliff's shaking hands plunked down an exorbitant price for the precious rolls of antacids from the resort gift and sundry store, he worried even more about pleasuring Mallory when his mind and body seemed to be functioning on altogether different tracks.

"OH, GOD, Mallory, I'm sorry." Cliff squirmed in the bed beside her. "This has never happened to me before."

Mallory rolled over and surveyed her embarrassed lover with a speculative expression. She propped her chin on her hands. "Cliff, it's all right. It doesn't matter."

He glared at her. "If you dare say it's no big thing—"

She couldn't help herself. A giggle—it was definitely a giggle—bubbled up. Hastily she primmed her mouth. "I would never say that. But it doesn't matter."

He groaned and put his forearm over his brow. "I'm in bed with one of the most desirable women I've ever met. She's smart. She's charming. She wants me. And I can't…"

"Appreciate your good fortune?"

"I just *can't,* all right?"

Mallory cuddled against him and put her head on his shoulder. Automatically, his arm curved around her side, pulling her closer. "Cliff, I'm the one who should apologize. You've been upset ever since we left home, haven't you?"

A soft grunt acknowledged her point.

"And I just sat in the car and chattered. I hardly let you get a word in edgewise."

Another soft grunt. But she noticed that some of the tension seeped out of his arm.

"Cliff, looking back it's obvious you had something you wanted to talk about. And I never gave you a chance. I'm sorry."

A long moment passed, marked only by the thudding of his heart against her cheek. Finally, he said, "Look, Mallory. Our affair was just for kicks, right? It wasn't meant for me to dump my troubles on you."

She sat up and punched him in the arm just hard enough to get his attention. Sure enough, that concealing forearm dropped, and he sat up and stared at her. "What was that for?"

"How dare you imply that I'm only interested in your body!"

"But that's what we agreed—"

"Maybe so, but I seem to remember someone who went out of his way to go beyond that for me. I remember a guy who listened to me rattle on about my hopes with the network job. A guy who made sure I felt genuinely desired when I got a little nervous the first time he kissed me. A guy who even took me bowling to help me forget a hellacious day. Does that sound like anyone you recognize?"

He blinked. "Well, yeah. I guess."

"So why should you think all that caring should go one direction only? Why should you have to do all that for me, while I do nothing for you?" She paused. "Look, Cliff. Just because we're only having an affair doesn't mean we can't care about each other, does it? Because if it does—if it does, I think I'd rather just have your friendship back again and forget the sex."

He blinked again, then a slow smile dawned. "You really aren't disappointed, are you?"

"Yes, I am. I'm disappointed that you thought you had to ignore your own problems just to keep me happy. I'm disappointed in myself for not being perceptive enough to realize that you're completely stressed out. And, yes, I'm disappointed that we're not going to be able to make love tonight." She leaned closer and cupped his face with her hands. "But there's no way I'm disappointed in *you*. Do you understand?"

"Yes, ma'am. Got it."

"Good." She lay down and pulled him beside her, settling back into a comforting cuddle. "So, why don't you tell me about whatever is making you eat antacids like popcorn? Maybe we can come up with some ideas to help solve the problem."

But though she paid strict attention to his careful explanation of the uncomfortable situation at work, one tiny corner of her mind contemplated what had just happened. Had she really told him she'd rather have his friendship than his lovemaking? And if so, whatever had happened to her determination to have a relationship that was purely physical, with none of the messy complications emotional ties always produced?

And why didn't she care that this affair that was supposed to be so physically satisfying and convenient for them both, had somehow transmuted into a relationship that was neither satisfying nor convenient?

# 7

CLIFF WOKE TO A feeling of restful contentment and with Mallory's warm body snuggled against him. For the first time in weeks he'd actually slept the night through. They'd talked long into the night—actually, he'd done most of the talking. Without getting into specifics, he'd managed to explain enough of his work dilemma for Mallory to offer some suggestions for how he might cope with it—beginning with scheduling a meeting with his boss as soon as he got back to the office.

To his surprise, he didn't feel upset or threatened by her knowing he was having problems with his career. She'd shared a few of her own harrowing job experiences, even admitting that she'd handled a couple of situations badly in earlier years.

Yup, having a woman he could really talk to as well as make love to was turning out to have all kinds of benefits.

That thought reminded him that they hadn't actually made love last night. He lay very still while he mentally checked himself out. Stomach okay? Not a sign of the churning pain he'd become so familiar with. Arms and legs? Nicely tangled with their female equivalents. Heart? Thumping out a heavy rhythm against the feminine palm draped over his chest. Mood? Relaxed, affectionate, definitely interested.

Horny, even.

As he began to stir and harden, he decided he really preferred early-morning love to the late-night kind, anyway. So what if he hadn't managed to do his part last night? This morning was another day, and based on what he was feeling now, it was time to give them both a little early-morning exercise.

Smiling with lecherous intent, he leaned over Mallory's sleeping face and nibbled delicately at her ear. ''Mallory? Honey? You awake?''

*''Mmmmph.''* But she turned toward his seeking lips.

Ever obliging, he changed his focus to her mouth. ''Wake up, honey.''

This time her response was slightly more verbal. ''Don' wanna. Havin' a good dream.''

His smile deepened. He bet he knew exactly what she was dreaming about. Especially since her arms had looped around his neck. ''You'll miss some good stuff if you don't wake up.''

One sleep-glazed eye popped open. "How good?" she asked suspiciously.

"*Really* good."

The other eye opened. "You promise?"

Deliberately, he let his lower body press against her so she could feel his burgeoning erection. "What do you think?"

Sleep melted from her eyes as she smiled contentedly. "I think I wouldn't want to miss anything that good."

Slowly, taking his time, he started to arouse her. It was fun discovering all his favorite places to linger on her body. They all smelled of Mallory's own heady aroma—light, yet musky; sweet, but definitely sensual. His heartbeat kicked into overdrive as he caressed and teased, tickled and soothed. And could there be anything headier than having her respond with equal heat? Or feeling her hands explore his own body? Or tasting her mouth with his? Or hearing her breathy gasps mixed with an urgent ringing. Why, he could almost hear bells...

Bells?

He froze. "Tell me that's not what I think it is."

Solemnly, she stared up at him, disappointment fogging over the arousal in her eyes. After a long moment, awareness kicked in and she groaned. "You did agree that we needed a wake-up call this morning."

The phone kept ringing.

With rueful intent, he said, "The next time I agree to anything so silly, I want you to kick me—hard." He reached over and grabbed the phone.

An obnoxiously sunny voice declared, "Good morning. This is your wake-up call. The time is six-thirty-two."

"Right," he groused. Clattering the phone back onto its rest, he stared at Mallory. "Where do they get these improbably cheerful people, anyway?"

She rolled out of bed, leaving him with only a lingering, wistful memory and the tempting sight of her, wrapped in the sheet, as she headed for the closet to grab some clothes. "I'll be out of the bath as soon as I can. I want to be at the station by eight."

"It'd be quicker if we shared," he offered, still with the faint hope of finishing what he'd started.

She looked at him over her shoulder, looking so adorably tousled that it was all he could do not to sweep her back into bed. "You're joking, right? If we shared, we'd still be here at noon—tomorrow."

Her words soothed his battered ego. The fates were conspiring against them, that was for sure. But with the determination of a man who had almost achieved nirvana, he vowed that this was the last time he would let the outside world interfere with his lovemaking with Mallory.

The very last time.

"WE NEVER SEEM to get a break, do we?" Cliff slickly maneuvered the car around someone determined to drive at sixty-five in the high-speed lane. Everyone else was breaking seventy. Despite their best intentions, it was after seven-thirty and Mallory hadn't yet made it to the station. Early-morning traffic tie-ups on Interstate 5 had sabotaged them. Having finally reached an open stretch of freeway, Cliff was taking advantage of it.

"No, we don't," she said. "Maybe someone's trying to tell us something."

"Like what?"

"Like maybe this affair idea wasn't such a good one." She swiveled in her seat as much as her seat belt would allow. "Cliff, we've been interrupted more times than a late-night movie has commercials. Maybe I was right the first time when I said that we should both just give up on having a relationship with anyone until after we're more established in our careers."

He glanced at her. "But I don't want to wait."

"Neither do I—but aren't you beginning to see a pattern?"

"What I'm seeing is that we need some serious time together. When we're at either of our condos, the phone and our pagers constantly interrupt. When we try to get away for a night, I bring enough of my work pressures with me that it interferes."

"So what's your conclusion, Counselor? That we should give up on each other and find partners without so many career demands?"

"No!" Cliff paused, not exactly sure himself where he was leading. Wherever it was, he was sure it didn't involve giving up Mallory—or having her start a relationship with someone else! Finally, he said slowly, "I think we need to make our relationship a priority, at least until we're comfortable with each other. Maybe go away somewhere without any phones or pagers or wake-up calls."

The look on her face was odd, closed, protecting her thoughts as she mulled over his suggestion. He had no idea what she was thinking. All he could really tell was that he'd surprised her. Hell, for that matter, he'd surprised himself! Never had he expected to tell any woman that being with her was a higher priority than his career.

*But I didn't mean we have to upset our priorities forever—only for right now. It's just until we can get this affair off the ground. Once we've established ourselves in our own minds as a couple, we can settle down to a comfortable time together. And our lives— my life—will be back on track.*

Yeah, that was it. They only needed perhaps a week or two together, long enough to scratch the itch that was driving him crazy, work that first urgent rush for each other out of their systems so they could concentrate on other, more important things. Once that driving need had been satisfied, he was sure they'd both be contented with occasional meetings when they could synchronize their schedules.

After all, that's the way they'd planned it in the first place. He had a career to manage and she had a network to impress.

He'd almost forgotten that she hadn't responded to his suggestion when she spoke up. ''What exactly are you suggesting?''

''Hell, I don't know. Maybe that we need to plan a getaway together—someplace where no one can get to us and we can truly be alone.'' Inspiration struck. ''How about up in Julian?'' The small gold-mining community in the mountains about an hour east of San Diego had transformed itself into a tourist mecca, popular for locals who simply wanted to get away from the daily grind for a while.

He still couldn't figure out what she was thinking. She'd make a damned good poker player. ''How long are you talking about for this getaway?''

''Two weeks?'' he suggested.

''Two weeks? Are you nuts? Sweeps month is coming up in a few weeks. And did you forget that I'm still waiting on the network's decision to schedule an interview with me? There's no way I can get away for that long.'' She paused. ''Maybe I could do another overnight or something, but...''

"Not enough time. Look what happened this time." His vague gesture encompassed their all-too-frustrating stay at the resort. "No, we'd need at least a week together."

She crossed her arms over her chest. "I don't see how I can be out of touch for a whole week."

Cliff reached over and took her hand. "Mallory, don't you think what we have is worth fighting for? Once we're settled in together, it's going to be great. I promise."

Her face softened but her voice didn't give quarter. "Seems to me you promised me something great for this morning, too."

He ignored that. "Give me a weekend. A long weekend together. We'll leave Friday morning, come back Monday morning. No pagers allowed. We won't tell anyone where we're going. It's only for one weekend. You can arrange that much time off, can't you?"

Slowly, she nodded. "A long weekend. I'll clear my calendar starting this Friday, all right?"

Second thoughts reared, reminding Cliff of his own schedule, crammed full of not-to-be-missed appointments. Ruthlessly, he shoved them aside. "Next weekend it is. I'll make reservations and we'll leave bright and early Friday morning. And don't forget we won't be back until late Monday."

Solemnly, they shook hands on their new deal.

THE PHONE IN Mallory's office rang with an insistent chirp. Despite the week's ill-omened start, she'd made it to Thursday without any serious problems. She'd managed to beg off work for Friday and had cleared her schedule. Of course, next week would be a bear because she'd have to cram in all Friday and Monday's appointments too, but she could live with that inconvenience for the sake of finally having Cliff all to herself.

The phone chirped again and Mallory picked it up.

"Mallory! It's me, Lenny."

As if she could ever mistake that booming voice. "Hi, Lenny. Everything going okay with you?"

He chuckled his I-know-something-you-don't chuckle. "Great, in fact. Hey, Mallory, what're you doing tomorrow?"

*Oh, no.* "Actually, I'm taking the day off." She took a deep breath. "Why?"

"That's wonderful! You always did have the most perfect timing." He paused for effect, making her ask.

"Okay, Lenny. Lay it on me. Why do you care what I do with my Friday?"

"Because, my favorite-client-of-all, tomorrow is the day the network honchos are coming to San Diego to meet with you personally."

*"What?"* Mallory's breath started coming in brief, gasping pants.

"You heard me. I got a call this morning. All of a sudden they've changed their minds about putting you off and decided they want to see you—now."

"But…but…" Her mind spinning with possibilities, she tried to figure out what this change of plan might mean. "Do you think they're serious about me? Give it to me straight, Lenny. Are they just jerking our chains?"

"Cross my heart and hope to have to eat cold hot dogs, this is the real thing. I think their negotiations with someone else fell through and they've decided to see what they've been missing in you."

"I don't know what to say."

"Just say you'll clear your calendar for tomorrow and be prepared to knock these guys' socks off."

Mallory stared down at her organizer notebook and flipped the pages to reach the one for Friday. Several appointments had been written in, but each had already been rescheduled to various days next week.

"My calendar's already cleared," she said slowly. The words "Julian with Cliff," stared up at her accusingly. When she'd arrived at the office on Monday she'd written them in herself in bright red ink. Usually she noted appointments in pencil, but for this one she'd used ink, convinced that nothing at all could make her change her plans.

"Perfect!" Lenny burbled in her ear. "You're to

meet them at eight o'clock for breakfast at the U.S. Grant Hotel downtown—you know where that is?''

''Lenny—'' Was she really going to—?

''They said you should plan to spend the day with them—and maybe into Saturday, too. This is going to be a real, in-depth discussion of their plans for the show and how you might fit in with what they want.''

''Lenny—''

''Trust me, kiddo, you'll do fine. I want you to wear that black suit you have—you know the one. It's a smasher and it'll show them you're a real classy lady.''

Mallory listened to Lenny rattle on about how to prepare for the meeting. What was she going to do? This was the chance of a lifetime for her. Surely Cliff would understand—wouldn't he? They could go away together another weekend. In fact, if this offer came through, she really would clear a whole week so she could devote herself just to enjoying some private time with him.

*And then you'll leave him for the bright lights of New York.*

''You got all that, Mallory?'' Lenny's voice showed a trace of anxiety, probably because she hadn't responded.

''Yes.'' She took a deep breath, ready to commit

herself. "Lenny, I'm thrilled that you managed to arrange this for me."

"I know, I know. I'm the best agent you've got, right? But you're okay with this, right?" His anxiety was increasing.

Her hand pressed over her heart, as if to control the thumping there. She opened her mouth to give him the reassurance he needed and the words popped out. "Lenny, I can't meet with them tomorrow."

*Ohmigod. Ohmigod. Ohmigod. What did I just say?*

Dead silence rang in her ears.

"What did you say?" Obviously, he didn't believe it either.

Now that she'd said it once, it was easier to repeat it. "I said, I can't meet them Friday—or Saturday. I have something else I have to do. It's very important to me."

"More important than getting an anchor spot on a prime-time network-news magazine? What's more important than that?"

*Being alone with my lover.* "Lenny, I can't explain. You know I wouldn't blow a meeting like this off unless I absolutely had to, don't you? Believe me, this is something I *have* to do."

She knew Lenny well enough to know he was busily twisting paper clips into useless knots. It was his favorite pastime when one of his clients frustrated him with their irrationality.

She heard him take several long, deep breaths. When he spoke, his voice was dark and serious. "Mallory, you're not sick are you? You're not going into the hospital or anything, right?"

His genuine concern for her warmed her cold hands. "No, Lenny, it's nothing like that. But I've already made a commitment for this weekend and I really can't break it. This is such short notice. I mean, Friday is *tomorrow*. Surely these guys will understand that my schedule is already full, and we can get together next week sometime?"

"Mallory, you don't seem to understand. These guys are coming to San Diego to see you. Everyone else they talked to had to go to them." His voice pleaded with her to reconsider. "How often do you get network guys knocking on your door?"

But those bright red words on her calendar wouldn't release her from her commitment to Cliff. She knew he needed the time away with her as much as she did. Sunday night's disaster had been a huge embarrassment for him—for any man—and she blamed herself for much of it. Her lack of sensitivity to his emotional state had only exacerbated his stress. She simply couldn't let him down again.

"Lenny, I can't do it. Call them back and see if they'll reschedule for another time." Rapidly she flipped through her calendar. ''Tell them any other time this month will do—I'll clear my calendar for them if they give me forty-eight hours notice. *But I can't see them this weekend.*''

''But—''

''We're wasting time, Lenny. I'm not going to change my mind. Please, just ask them to reschedule and let me know what they say. Please.''

Her agent was disgruntled, but eventually agreed. Mallory sat for a long time staring at her organizer, wondering what madness had made her sacrifice everything she'd been working toward for the sake of a far-from-simple affair.

# 8

"ALONE AT LAST." Cliff uttered the heartfelt cliché with a sigh of relief. "You know, there were times I didn't think we'd make it here."

Mallory glanced at him as she dumped her overnight bag on a chair. Cliff had borrowed a small getaway home from a friend. It consisted of only a bedroom, a living area, and a small kitchen, and was nestled in the mountains within a half mile of Julian's short main street. Best of all, it had no phone service, though both the plumbing and electricity were fully operational.

"I know what you mean," she said. "But we're here. Pagerless. Phoneless. And, as far as I know, absolutely no one knows where we are."

He dumped the last of their various bags and provisions on the battered wooden table that served as both kitchen work area and dining table. "Did you have any trouble clearing your schedule?"

Mallory hesitated. She hadn't mentioned her agent's urgent call yesterday to Cliff for reasons she wasn't quite able to articulate, even to herself. "No," she said slowly, "not any more than I expected. How about you?"

He stuffed some perishables into the ancient refrigerator before answering. "Same here." Having successfully completed his task, he turned to her. "So. What would you like to do first?"

Involuntarily, her gaze focused on the doorway that led to the bedroom. She'd already checked it out and discovered the only truly luxurious piece of furniture in the entire cabin—a king-size bed covered with a fluffy comforter and a pile of soft pillows.

When their eyes met again, Cliff knew he'd been right to insist on this private getaway. Slowly, wanting to savor every second, he walked over to her. "It's time, isn't it?"

She never broke his gaze. "Yes," she said softly. "More than time."

But he had one more worry. "Mallory, this is what you want, too—isn't it?"

"Did you think I've changed my mind?" A smile licked the corners of her mouth, tilting it upwards just enough to entice.

"I haven't been sure. So many things have gone wrong between us. I thought maybe you were disappointed, or maybe just—"

"Shhh." Her fingers covered his mouth. "We went through that before."

His hands settled naturally at her waist, like a nesting bird settling into a well-hollowed space. "God knows I don't want to talk about it any more. But I don't want you to feel rushed."

He saw her smile widen first in those bluebell eyes. "I don't feel rushed. If anything, I feel like maybe I was right the first time."

"Right? About what?" He was memorizing her face. The tiny mole beside her left eyebrow, usually covered with makeup. The slightly asymmetrical arch of her eyebrows. The welcome in her smile.

"When I said you lawyers were all talk, no action." She looped her arms around his neck. "Why don't we forget all the what-ifs and maybes and just do what we came here to do?"

And though his arms tightened around her, Cliff couldn't quite let go of his worry. "This is going to be special. I'm going to make it special for you." He intended his words as a vow.

Only when he led her into the curtain-shadowed bedroom did she answer, a response that left him breathless. "Don't you understand, Cliff? It's already special because it's with you."

SHADOWS AND LIGHT permeated the room, glistening briefly on a gracefully feminine arm here, a sensuously tensed shoulder there. Their first moves were slow, tentative. Cliff helped Mallory undress, taking his time, treasuring each revelation. Then Mallory did the same, bestowing lingering caresses on his arms, chest, legs.

By the time they lay on that enormous, voluptuous bed, he'd forgotten why he had fretted so about his ability to please her. She was the most intensely responsive lover he'd ever had. Alone with him, protected from interruptions, she displayed a sensual enjoyment of his lovemaking that was utterly erotic.

He quickly forgot his worry that she would find him—or the circumstances—unsatisfactory yet again. Instead, he concentrated on drawing out both their pleasure, needing more than anything to demonstrate to her how very much he wanted her—and how much he wanted her to want him.

Wanting him didn't seem to be a problem. With her lips kissed to a rosy glow and the gleam of arousal in her eyes, she responded to his every movement. Sometimes she initiated her own arousing caresses, sometimes she followed his sensual lead as they rediscovered the age-old, ever-changing dance of completion. Her lips traced the outline of his body as ardently as his traced hers. Her hands touched and probed and explored with delight, just as he reveled in his explorations of her. Her body melded itself to his with eager passion that wordlessly conveyed her own pleasure.

And when he entered her, he thought he'd come home.

No, it was better than coming home. He lay for long, thundering heartbeats, buried deep inside her, half-afraid any movement would shatter this unbelievable sensation of utter *rightness*. He'd never experienced anything like it. In Mallory's arms he felt truly loved and wanted.

With his heart thumping out a drumbeat of desire, he slowly began to move, guiding Mallory's hips to his rhythm. He watched her face intently, waiting for the first signs of her release. Only when she called his name in a hoarse moan and he felt her quivering response surround him did he allow his own passion to erupt into a climax that splintered him into a million shards, then, somehow, amazingly, made him whole again.

"WAS IT GOOD FOR YOU?" Mallory's husky, teasing words feathered over his shoulder in sleepy humor.

He'd just managed to catch his breath from their latest bout of Olympic-class sex. If this kept up, he'd be dead by Sunday night. Ecstatic, but dead.

"Couldn't you tell?" Idly, he stroked her arm, tracing the muscles from shoulder to wrist. "If it was any better, I'd have died and gone to heaven." He paused. "What about for you?"

She must have sensed that his query wasn't made

in jest, but her voice was laced with satiated humor. "I *did* die and go to heaven. Didn't you see me sprouting my wings?"

"Wings, huh?" He ran his hands over her shoulder blades. He just couldn't stop stroking her skin, as smooth and warm as molasses left out in the sun. "I don't feel any feathers."

"That's because they all fell off when you dragged me back to earth."

"Dragged? I figured it was you dragging me. Weren't those your hands clutching my butt?"

She giggled, letting her breath tickle his cheek. "Caught. I guess I'll have to throw myself on the mercy of the court. Again."

He adopted a judicial frown and nestled her more firmly against him. "Well, Ms. Reissen, since this is your second offense, I'll have to be more strict with you. I sentence you…"

Suddenly, she rolled over, landing full length on top of him. "Sentence me to what?"

"Ahem. Young lady, what exactly do you think you're doing?" It was hell trying to maintain a properly judicious attitude with a naked nymph undulating against him.

"Throwing myself on your mercy?" She wriggled into a more intimate position.

"That's not my 'mercy' you're on."

"Oh. Well…it'll do, won't it?"

"Yes," he gasped as her squirming enticed his flagging body back into life. "It'll definitely *do*."

BUT THEY COULDN'T make love all the time. Eventually they decided to get out and enjoy their stay in Julian. After a hilarious shared shower and quickly made sandwiches eaten at the rickety table, they wandered outside. The day was perfect for mid-April. Bright blue skies domed over a forest rich with the scent of pine trees and resurgent spring growth. Delicate mountain wildflowers painted sheltered corners with purples and pinks and blues. And on nearly every sun-splashed bank, hordes of yellow daffodils proudly waved in the breeze from bulbs originally planted but now allowed to spread in wild profusion.

"It reminds me of my grandmother's home," Mallory commented as they walked contentedly into Julian's minuscule downtown area. "She lived up in the Sierras, and every spring her yard had tons of wildflowers blossoming everywhere."

Cliff looked at her curiously. "I had the impression that you were raised back east, not in the mountains of California."

She turned to stare into the antiques displayed in a store window. "Mostly I was in boarding schools. My parents were always busy with their careers, so that was the easiest option."

He sensed something more behind her careful explanation. Delicately, he probed. "Easiest for whom? Them? Or you?"

She tossed her head, letting the blond strands he'd persuaded her to leave free fly across her face and conceal her eyes. "Oh, both, I think. My mother is an archaeologist and is forever off on digs in really remote places—especially in summer during school vacations. And my father is a concert pianist who spends most of his time on world tours."

Cliff chewed that over for a moment. "Sounds like they weren't home much," he finally said carefully.

"They weren't. But then, neither was I." She flicked back that strand of hair and met his gaze head-on.

"What about vacations? Did you ever travel with your parents then?" He guided her around a pair of tourists, stepping into the recessed doorway of another shop.

"Oh, no. What would a kid do in Eastern Europe? You can't just let a ten-year-old wander around unsupervised in a foreign city. And my mother's digs were generally in places you wouldn't want to take a child. No, I stayed home with my Gramma Lawrence."

He could think of a lot of things a child could learn and enjoy in Europe—or even in remote areas, on an archaeological dig. Funny. He'd always thought of his own childhood as deprived, but at least his mother, unsatisfactory as she'd been as a parent and family breadwinner, had cared enough to keep him with her. It couldn't have been easy for her to raise him by herself. While she wasn't the greatest mother in the world, at least somewhere inside he'd always known she wanted him. And that validated the feelings of loss he'd experienced at eighteen when she'd died, a broken and bitter woman who never had the chance to make it big.

It wasn't much consolation, but it was something.

"Want some pie?" He gestured at the etched-glass windows of Mom's, one of the several pie shops that, according to the Julian chamber of commerce, made the best apple pies anywhere. When she nodded, he opened the door and led her inside. It wasn't until he'd collected two orders of apple-cherry pie with coffee and seated her at a table that something clicked in his memory.

"Is that the same Gramma Lawrence you were talking about last Sunday in the car? The one who left you some kind of legacy?"

"Mmm-hmm." She took a bite of the pie. "This is really good." After swallowing, she added, "I inherited her house up in Sunfield. It's where I spent all my summers and school vacations until she died when I was twelve. It's beautiful up there. I had a great time with Gramma. I'll probably have to sell the house, though. If I get that network job, or any network job really, I'll be based in New York, not California.''

Her casual statement was like a punch in his gut. *If she gets the network job, she'll be leaving for New York.* He knew that, of course. He'd always known she'd be leaving sooner or later. So why did that realization affect him so strongly now? She was too smart and too talented not to get what she wanted professionally.

He took a sip of coffee to moisten a mouth suddenly too dry. ''Do you think you're likely to hear something soon? About the New York job, I mean.''

She gave him an odd look he had no clue how to interpret. ''Maybe,'' she said. ''But we're having trouble scheduling a mutually convenient interview. It's possible they'll hire someone else without even talking to me.''

*She'll stay!* He tried to disguise the bubble of elation that rose at the thought. ''Oh. That's too bad.''

She changed the subject. But while they wandered and shopped desultorily in Julian's tiny downtown area, Cliff felt as if he'd successfully dodged a bullet. Mallory was going to stay in town, at least for a while longer, and he could simply concentrate on enjoying their time together.

But he soon urged her to return to the cabin, where he made love to her all afternoon and into the evening.

CLIFF ENJOYED taking Mallory out to dinner on Sunday evening. They settled on a local restaurant and lingered over the meal, holding hands and staring into each other's eyes. It amused him to realize that anyone watching them would have taken them for a honeymoon couple. And that thought surprised him. He'd have expected to be embarrassed or irritated at such an assumption.

As dessert was served, he realized to his surprise that neither of them had shown the slightest inclination to discuss their jobs. In fact, the words *career* and *work* had been tacitly taboo for almost the entire weekend, as if both were trying to forget that such real-world issues existed.

It was the longest period in years that he hadn't even thought about his work.

But as Mallory dipped her spoon into her caramel flan, she asked, "I've been meaning to ask you how your meeting with your boss went last week. Did you clear up the problems that were bothering you?"

Cliff's gaze released hers and he shifted uncomfortably. "I guess. I understand better now why they're doing what they're doing." His answer was deliberately vague because he hadn't been able to tell Mallory anything specific about his problems—and especially not that they related to the infamous Bartlett murder case.

Actually the senior partner had been very sympathetic about Cliff's concerns, but had pointed out the hard facts. Client fees paid for the salaries and office expenses of the firm, and clients who were sent to jail often were irritated enough not to pay their bills. Not to mention that they often bad-mouthed their attorneys to everyone who would listen, which wasn't very good for business. Besides, it was in the honored tradition of American jurisprudence that every client—even one with tons of evidence against her— be provided with the best possible defense.

Cliff did understand. He always had. He wasn't one of those pie-in-the-sky dreamers who dashed around tilting at windmills and making everyone— especially themselves—miserable.

But this case still seemed different. The cop in question was a good cop, with an excellent record of more than twenty years of work. He had a wife and a couple of kids. No doubt the hatchet job Cliff's firm planned would hurt, maybe even destroy, the man's career. And his family.

"That didn't sound very certain," Mallory commented on his less-than-enthusiastic agreement.

"It wasn't. I still disagree with the tactics." No, he *hated* the tactics. And surprised himself once again for caring. "It's funny. All your life you work for something and then when you get it, it turns out to be very different from what you expect."

Her head tipped sideways, considering his words. "What do you mean?"

"Only that real life is different from what you see in movies or read in books." He gestured vaguely. "As a kid I saw all those rich, successful lawyers riding around in great cars and living in ritzy houses, and I thought, man, that's the place to be."

"And isn't it?" Her question was gently put, and her fingers closed around his.

"Not really." He gave a wry grin. "I never realized that if you're going to make money defending people from criminal charges, you end up spending a lot of your time hanging around with criminals."

"You mean your clients aren't all lily-white?" she teased.

"God, no. Some are merely rich enough to buy their way out of trouble."

He saw the question gathering in her eyes before she asked it. "Then how can you defend them if you know they're guilty?"

His lips twisted into a wry grin. "Because we're trained in law school that everyone—even the guilty—is entitled to a defense. Besides, I don't *know* they're guilty—we're also trained never to ask that question. Guilt or innocence is for the jury to decide."

She shook her head, but changed the subject. "Tomorrow's Monday. We have to go home then."

He nodded. "I know."

She shoved her dessert aside and stared at him through the golden candlelight. "I don't want to go back."

"Neither do I." It was true. Even the thought of facing the same problems again made his stomach clench.

Her wistful smile tugged at his heart. "I don't suppose you'd like to run away with me, would you? We'd never have to go back to the real world."

With all his heart he wanted to say yes. "Sorry. You'd miss out on your grand career plan. The network is waiting for you, you know. And I wouldn't make partner."

For a long heartbeat she stared at him. "And would that be so bad?"

"It's what you want, what you've always wanted. Isn't it?"

She studied his face for a moment without answering. Then she released his hand and pushed away from the table. "We'd better be going."

Her words were said with the finality of an epitaph. He knew she was right. It was time to leave this idyllic interlude and return to the things that really mattered. Their careers.

Their affair was well established now. They were comfortable with each other in bed and out. They had a genuine "relationship," a word which sent instinctive shivers up his bachelor spine but which also seemed right when it referred to him and Mallory.

Yes, this weekend had accomplished everything he'd wanted it to. So why was he so reluctant to put it behind him and return to what he truly loved?

# 9

LENNY'S VOICE abraded Mallory's ear. "They canceled, Mallory. They've found someone else."

It was three weeks since she'd returned from the trip into the mountains, and she'd kept the hope alive that her impulsiveness hadn't destroyed her chance to hit the big time. Obviously, those hopes were in vain.

She sank into her office chair and propped her forehead on one hand. "Are you sure? They didn't leave any possibility open that they'll change their minds again?"

"Not a chance. I won't repeat their exact words, but the general implication of their comments was 'unreliable.' You wouldn't do what they wanted and they were, uh, really irritated."

Absently, Mallory noticed that her hand was shaking. She stared at it as if it were an alien object. "That's that, I guess. Bye-bye golden network opportunity."

"Aw, kid, don't take it hard. Another chance'll

come up. Besides, I heard some rumors about this project I don't think you'd like.''

''Rumors?'' One of the many things she adored about her agent was his loyalty. ''What are you talking about?''

Lenny dropped his voice to what he probably supposed was a whisper. It actually meant she could hold the receiver against her ear in comfort. ''I heard this prime-time slot is for a real sleazoid tabloid show. Not in the news division at all—in the entertainment group. Don't know how well you'd have liked that.''

She really appreciated his attempts to cheer her up, so she went along with his story. ''You're probably right, Lenny. I wouldn't have liked that much at all.''

''Don't worry. We'll find something better for you pretty soon now.''

Mallory said goodbye to her agent and hung up. It was just like Lenny to do his best for her, even when she'd been the one to let him down.

Doodling on a pad of paper, she contemplated her future. At the moment, it didn't look like much except a series of empty days and even emptier nights. Even her affair with Cliff had deteriorated since their return from Julian. He worked so much that they'd only managed to be together three times. And each time, he'd left her bed in the early morning before she awakened, leaving her feeling lonelier than before.

Maybe she wasn't cut out for an affair.

Maybe she wasn't cut out for the "big time," either. Certainly those network guys seemed to think that was the case.

She stared at her organizer where she'd penciled in dinner with Cliff for that evening. The truth was, she wasn't really depressed over losing out on the network show. After three weeks of delays and stalling tactics, she'd known in her heart that this time she wouldn't get that job. She was a big girl now, and she had to take the consequences of choosing a weekend with Cliff over a last-minute interview with the network.

While she regretted the lost professional opportunity, she spent far more time fretting over her relationship with Cliff. She wanted more than just an occasional evening in bed together. He was a tender, caring lover, to be sure, but when he disappeared even before the sun rose, she ended up feeling slightly used instead of satisfied.

The phone chirped, interrupting her disgruntled ponderings. "Mallory Reissen."

"Hi. It's Cliff."

"I was just thinking about you," she said. Her heart thumped heavily at the sound of his voice. "I'm really glad you called."

"Good." Papers rustled in the background. "I wanted to talk to you about dinner."

Ignoring the warning frisson that shuddered down her spine, she said quickly, "Would you like to try that new Japanese place? Someone here at work said their sushi is outstanding."

"Mallory—"

Bowing to the inevitable, she let him interrupt her. A sinking feeling in her stomach prepared her for his words.

"I can't make dinner tonight. I've got to work."

*Damn, damn, damn.* It was the fifth time in two weeks he'd canceled a date with her. *But that's what you agreed to, dummy. You were going to be sympathetic and understanding when he has to work. Just as he's been when you had to cancel.*

True enough, but she'd only canceled once, when a huge fire raced through a downtown high-rise.

"Mallory? Are you there?".

"Yes." Her voice wasn't as controlled as she liked, so she cleared her throat. "I'm here."

"Look, honey, I'm really sorry. But I think this might be a major break for me. I have to get this work done tonight, but I'm hoping it'll get me noticed."

She cleared her throat again and blinked quickly. "That's—that's all right, Cliff. I understand. Would you like me to have something ready to heat up when

you come in?'' One of their few evenings together
had resulted from just such an offer. Cliff had arrived
shortly before midnight, he'd gobbled down the re-
heated meat loaf she'd saved, and they'd gone to bed.
Of course, the next morning he was up and gone
before six.

"No," he said, regret lacing his voice. "I'll probably be here into the wee smalls. I'll just send one
of the clerks out for a sandwich or something."

"Oh."

"I'm really sorry about this. I know you were
looking forward to dinner. I was, too."

Determinedly, she raised her chin. Sheer pride was
keeping her going and strengthening her voice to a
calm firmness. "Never mind. There'll be other evenings." *Wouldn't there?* "You get your work done
and we'll see each other another time."

But after she'd ended the call she stared at the
phone for long moments. The temptation to sweep it
off the desk onto the floor was nearly irresistible—
she had to curl her fingers until her nails stung her
palms to prevent such a foolish action.

Her anger built into a flame that flickered higher.
A quick rap at the door to her office sent her slewing
around.

"Hey, Mallory, here's the latest from the boss on
the sweeps results. We're doing really well so far.
Up three points in the 24-to-35 age group." Janet

Powell, one of the station administrators, held out a memo to her. Janet and she occasionally shared a lunch at a local deli on slow news days. She was also the only person at the station who knew anything at all about Mallory's relationship with Cliff.

It took three deep breaths before Mallory could respond. ''Good. That's good.''

''Good? Girl, that's great. And most of the uptick seems to be a direct result of your series on traffic problems and population growth. People were really interested in what you presented.''

''Terrific.'' A pounding headache was starting just behind her left eye.

Janet stared at her, then walked the rest of the way into the office and shut the door. ''All right, what's wrong?''

She could have evaded the question. She even seriously considered lying. But at this moment, she needed to talk to someone. Janet was sympathetic. In her mid-forties, she'd also been around long enough to have useful advice.

''It's Cliff,'' Mallory confessed. ''He just canceled another dinner date.''

Drawing up the visitor's chair and planting her ample backside in it, Janet asked, ''What is this? The third time, lately?''

''The fifth.'' Even saying the words made it sound worse.

"You think he's cheating on you?" That was Janet. Go straight to the heart of the matter.

"No. Except maybe with his work. He's just more devoted to it than to me."

"So he's got his work as a mistress, right?"

"No," Mallory said slowly. "*I'm* his mistress. His work is his wife."

"Honey, one thing I've learned is that the wife usually wins. Playing the other woman is like betting against the house. Sooner or later, it's going to clean you out."

"But I promised him I wouldn't come between him and his work. It was what we agreed to." Even Mallory could hear the wail in her voice.

"Why'd you agree to something silly like that?"

The question stopped her cold. Why *had* she agreed to it? Her reasons seemed remote and vague now, though she clearly remembered proposing the terms of their affair to Cliff herself. Why would she want a relationship in which she didn't even get to see her partner except occasionally? Why would she want a relationship just like her—

"Ohmigod."

"What is it?"

"I'm living my parents' life. They're really involved in their careers, barely are in the same city for more than a few weeks a year. Somehow, I've begun to model my life after theirs."

"Doesn't sound right to me." Janet thought about it. "Is that the life you really want for yourself? Waiting around for the man you love to toss you a crumb of his time?"

"Love? Who said anything about love?" Though she leaped to deny it, the heat of truth crept up her neck.

"Mallory, honey, I've known you for years. I've seen you date tons of guys—great guys. But I've never seen you so heated up over anyone. If this isn't love, I don't know what is."

"But—" Mallory shut up. Janet's unerring eye had revealed what she'd hidden from herself. She wasn't just resentful of Cliff's job. She wanted him to turn his attention to her because she wanted his love. She wanted him not to work so hard. She wanted him to eat more regularly, get more rest.

Be with her more.

She'd broken the biggest rule of all. She'd fallen head over heels for a man who didn't have time to love.

PETER ABRAMS, senior partner at Abrams, Dentwhistle, Farber, and Cox, patted Cliff on the shoulder. "Excellent work, Cliff. You've really done us proud."

Cliff tried to look appropriately humble. "I like to make a contribution to the firm."

"Well, we've all seen how hard you've worked on helping us prepare the Bartlett case. With the trial date now set for late June, it's time to fire up the defense team. My partners and I feel you'll be a great asset to us."

Cliff blinked. For all his misgivings about the defense strategy, this was still a major coup. A case like this would be a career-maker. Especially if they won. Still, he might have misunderstood. "You mean—"

"I mean that as of this afternoon you're officially part of the defense team for Fiona Bartlett." Abrams stuck out his hand. "Congratulations, Cliff."

Dazed, Cliff shook the older man's hand. Perhaps it was the combination of too little sleep and too much work. Or maybe it was simply the impact of being the only nonpartner included in the prestigious defense team. In either event, he walked back to his office in a daze, collecting congratulations as he went. He'd done it! He'd actually done it.

His first thought was to call Mallory. He'd felt bad about blowing off their dinner date yet again. These last few weeks he hadn't seen nearly as much of her as he'd have liked. Still, their time in the mountains had accomplished what he'd hoped, and he'd been able to attack his work with renewed vigor and enthusiasm ever since. Which had resulted, of course, in today's victory. In a way, he could credit Mallory for all this—and he couldn't think of a better way to celebrate than by taking her to bed.

"Mallory Reissen."

"Me again." The big sappy grin on his face wouldn't turn off. He twirled in his chair like a little kid.

"Cliff! I thought you were working late tonight."

"I was, but I decided to take the night off. I'm shoving all the paperwork into the circular file and shuffling out of here at a reasonable hour tonight."

A wary silence filled his ear. "What brought this on?"

"I'll tell you tonight. You can make it after all, can't you?"

"Well…to be honest, since you couldn't meet me for dinner I agreed to help out on a promo spot after the evening news. I won't be able to leave until at least eight or eight-thirty."

"That's okay," he said easily. "I have some stuff to do here before I can leave anyway. Why don't I meet you at the restaurant at nine? After we eat, we'll go home and get naked."

To his surprise, she didn't leap at the offer. Had he been mistaken when he thought she'd been disappointed at his earlier cancellation for tonight? "Cliff, maybe we should do this another night," she said at last. "I'm going to be pretty tired."

*What was going on here? Didn't she want to be with him?* "Mallory, is anything wrong?"

"No." Her voice sounded tired. Maybe she was merely feeling a little stressed. "All right," she capitulated. "But let's not go out. I'll stop by a take-out place and bring some food with me. I think we need some privacy, to talk."

"Great!" His mood restored, he sent her a smacking kiss over the phone line. "I'll see you around nine at my place. And, Mallory—prepare to celebrate, big-time. I've got some great news to share."

"I've got news, too," she said so quietly he barely noticed.

Idly, he wondered what her news was, then dismissed the question. He'd find out this evening. Meantime, he had six hours to finish up the paperwork cluttering his desk and get himself home. With renewed vigor, he pulled his legal pad toward him, flipped to a clean sheet, and started making notes.

MALLORY KNOCKED on Cliff's front door with her arms full of chicken lo mein and chopsticks. Nervously, she moistened her lips. This evening was going to be very difficult.

Ever since her revelation with Janet, she'd been trying to figure out what to do about Cliff. Did she want to continue a relationship that was inherently self-destructive for her? Could she bear to walk away from him?

Truthfully, she didn't know.

The door was flung open and Cliff pulled her inside, giving her a huge kiss and hug. "God, you look gorgeous!"

She handed him the bags of food and slipped out of the light jacket she wore against the early evening chill. "Sorry I'm so late. The promo spots took a little longer than I expected."

"Never mind. You're here now. I've got the table set and the wine's poured. Let's dish up the food and eat."

Silently she let him lead her to the dining area. Once they were served, she asked, "I gather something good happened at work this afternoon?" Maybe if she let him get his good news out first, he'd be in a mood to talk about their relationship.

He put down his chopsticks with a smile that threatened to split his face. "You might say that. As of today I am now officially a member of the Bartlett defense team. The one and only nonpartner so honored, I might add."

*Oh, no.* She knew what this meant. Instead of him being able to make more time to be together, the all-out effort for this trial would cut even further into his nearly nonexistent free time. Still, he was obviously looking for approval. "Cliff, that's wonderful.

I'm thrilled for you.'' Okay, so ''thrilled'' was an exaggeration. She genuinely was pleased he'd achieved what he'd worked so hard to get.

''This is going to be my ticket to the paneled offices, Mallory. They only wanted one junior member of the firm on the team—Fiona Bartlett always wants only the best of the best—and I'm the one they chose. I can hardly believe it.''

She leaned forward and took his hand. ''Cliff, there's not a doubt in my mind that you deserve this. You've been working so hard lately. They must have noticed your dedication.''

Smugly, he nodded, and regaled her with the details of how everyone in the office had reacted when the news was announced. Only when he was winding down did he appear to notice that she'd contributed little to the conversation.

''Mallory, didn't you say you have some news, too?''

She smiled weakly. ''It can't compare with yours, I'm afraid. It's just—the network isn't interested in me, after all.''

''What? I didn't even know you'd interviewed with them.'' Automatically, he shoved their plates aside so he could grasp her hand more tightly in his.

''I didn't. They wanted to talk to me the weekend we went up to Julian, but…well, I already had other plans. Since then, we've been getting the old run-around trying to schedule a meeting.'' She shrugged. ''Lenny says they've now settled on someone else.''

''Why didn't you talk with them that weekend? I would have understood.''

She looked down at their clasped hands. ''I decided I didn't want to cancel our weekend together. I thought it was important—you thought it was then, too.''

''Yes, but this was your chance at the networks. I would never have stood in your way for that!'' He looked profoundly shocked at the thought.

''I know that, Cliff. It was my decision, not yours.''

''I just don't understand. Why would you deliberately ruin your own chances like that?''

He'd moved the conversation to the one area she both needed to discuss and dreaded bringing up. She took a deep breath and came to a decision. ''Before I answer that, will you tell me something?''

''Of course.''

''Will your new position on the defense team mean more work for you—or less?''

His surprise couldn't have been faked. ''More, of course. As a member of the team, I'll have to double-check everything. I won't just be producing briefs, I'll be responsible for their accuracy and timeliness. I'll be working harder than ever.''

''That's what I thought.'' Her fingers clutched his

so tightly her knuckles ached. "Cliff, I want to end our relationship now, tonight."

"*What?*"

"Remember we said in the beginning that if I ever wanted out, all I had to do was tell you and that would be the end of it? Well, I'm telling you. I want out."

"But—Mallory—*why?* What's wrong? Whatever it is, let's talk about it. Surely we can fix it."

Her free hand came up to thread through his hair. "You said you'd never stand in the way of my career. You told me you'd support me in my decisions."

He paled. "Are you telling me you're going to New York after all? I thought you said the network job fell through."

She shook her head. "No. I'm saying I can't be so generous as that with you. I want nothing more than to tell you I don't want you taking on the Bartlett case. I don't want you working harder than you already are—in fact, I want you to ease up, work fewer hours." She took a breath that was more of a swallowed gulp. "I want you to have more time for me."

"I don't understand."

"Don't you see, Cliff? I'm as bad as Suzanne and all the other women you've known. I want more from you than an hour in bed when you can fit me in between your clients. If we don't break this off now, you'll grow to dislike me, just as you've disliked all those other women who were too demanding of your time and energy. And I can't stand the thought of that.''

"Mallory, I thought things were going well between us. Why can't we—''

His face dissolved in the mist of tears she refused to let fall. "Don't you get it, Cliff? I'm in love with you. I want all of you, not just the little pieces you're willing to share. I know I can't have that. It's not in you to love me. But at least I can leave before I make you hate me. That's why I have to go.''

Of course he argued. Cliff refused to believe that a compromise couldn't be worked out. But to his frustration, she stood firm against all his arguments. No, she wouldn't reconsider. No, she wouldn't change her mind.

No, she wouldn't stay.

In the end, he had to accept defeat. Not graciously. Not willingly. But he had to accept it nonetheless.

He won only one concession from her. She agreed to spend the night with him. He thought if he made love to her as tenderly and thoroughly as he knew how, she would understand how much she meant to him. And then her compassionate heart would realize how hurt he was that she wanted to leave him.

So they shared one last, loving farewell, a fitting

epitaph for an affair that had been nothing but in-
convenient from the very first day.

And when he woke before dawn, she was already
gone.

# *10*

---

FOR THE TENTH time in the past week, Cliff picked up his office phone to call Mallory. His door was shut. His secretary had left two hours ago, at five-thirty. As far as he knew, only the janitors shared the office with him this Friday night. He was as safe from discovery as he could be.

This time, he actually punched in the numbers with fingers that trembled. Four soft rings later, he was almost certain he'd waited too late and she'd already left the station for the day.

"Mallory Reissen."

The sound of her voice, the first time he'd heard it in over a month, sucked the air from his lungs. He couldn't make a sound.

"Hello? Hello?"

*She was about to hang up.* "Don't hang up, Mallory. It's Cliff."

She was silent so long he wasn't sure she hadn't hung up anyway. "Hello, Cliff."

Now what? "I, uh, just wanted to know if you were all right. I've been thinking about you."

"I'm fine." While not impolite, the chill courtesy in her voice could have frozen a Popsicle.

"Oh. I'm fine, too."

"Good."

Had a more inane conversation ever taken place? He hadn't felt so inept since he was a thirteen-year-old requesting his first date. Which thought at least reminded him of his reason for calling.

"Mallory, I've been wondering. Would you like to go to dinner sometime soon? Maybe take in a movie?"

He measured her hesitation in heartbeats. Four long, thudding pumps later, she sighed. "Cliff, I don't think that's a very good idea."

"Please, Mallory. I'd like to see you."

"You see me all the time. I live right next door, remember?"

He ignored that. "Please."

Three. Four. This time it took five heartbeats for her to respond. "Are you still on the Bartlett defense team?"

"Yes, of course."

She sighed audibly. "Then I don't think it's a very good idea to start things up again between us, do you?"

"Dammit, Mallory, are you trying to punish me for being successful at what I do?"

"No, Cliff," she said gently. "I'm trying *not* to punish myself. That's all."

With a soft click, the phone went dead. Slowly, Cliff dropped the handset onto its cradle. With a groan that was torn painfully from his gut, he buried his head in his hands and stayed that way for a long, long time.

FIONA BARTLETT draped herself over the conference-room chair with the suppleness of a panther. She looked a lot like a panther, Cliff thought. All long, sleek lines and hungry eyes.

Unfortunately, the meal she hungered for seemed to be him.

"Cliff—you don't mind if I call you Cliff, do you?" Even her voice was a husky purr.

"Not at all, Ms. Bartlett. Cliff is fine."

"I was just wondering why I haven't had the opportunity to meet with you before now. The trial is about to start and I feel it's important that everyone on my team be on my side."

He rubbed his chin and wondered where the hell the paralegal was. He was sure he'd instructed her to be in the conference room at three o'clock on the dot. A quick glance at his watch confirmed it was now ten minutes after the hour.

Through some careful maneuvering and some plain, dumb luck, he'd managed to avoid being alone with the predatory Mrs. Bartlett until now. Apparently, his luck had run out. Along with that useless paralegal.

"We have met, of course," he said as smoothly as he could manage. *In large groups where I could be sure you were under control.* "And I'm only a very minor member of your team—more a support person than anything else. Hardly important enough to waste your time with."

She frowned and leaned sideways just enough to give him a glimpse of long, dark-stockinged leg stretched in voluptuous enticement. "But I thought you had something important to go over with me."

"I do," he assured her, ignoring her scarlet-painted pout. "But if you'll excuse me, I'll round up our paralegal. She has copies of the paperwork we need to go over."

"But—"

Before she could protest, Cliff slipped out the door. Hastily he stepped to a nearby secretary's station. "Where the hell is Lucy? She was supposed to be here—"

"Sorry, Mr. Young!" Lucy Davenwood dashed up, her arms full of papers and files. "Mrs. Bartlett told me on her way in that she needed at least a half

hour in private consultation with you, so I thought I
should—''

Of course. By this time Fiona Bartlett must know
enough of the workings of her attorneys' office to
know exactly how to sabotage his plans to avoid being alone with her.

Resigned, he just nodded. ''That's all right. You're
here now.'' He took a stack of papers from her and
guided her to the closed conference room door. ''But,
Lucy, no matter what she says, you don't leave this
room unless I tell you it's all right—understood?''

She nodded earnestly.

Grim-faced, he stepped back inside the lioness's
den to discuss the depositions he'd been assigned to
review with her. Was this what he really wanted to
do with his life? Play dodgem with predatory women
and defend them in court from the consequences of
their own actions?

In his own mind he'd long ago realized that Fiona
Bartlett wasn't merely guilty—she was as guilty as
sin. From his reading of the evidence, she hadn't
found her husband in bed with another woman and
shot the pair in a rage. No, all the evidence pointed
to a very carefully planned setup of both her husband
and his lover—a woman who had once been Fiona's
best friend.

And he was bound by oath to help Fiona walk free.

His hand groped in his pocket for the antacids that

were once again a staple of his diet. How he longed for Mallory's presence to help him sort through his life! She had a deep-rooted rational approach to sticky problems that he needed desperately. Yet after that one futile phone call, she'd started screening her calls both at work and at home. And messages from C. Young went mysteriously unanswered.

He never saw her entering or leaving her condo, though he made a point of looking for her whenever he was home—which was seldom. And just lately he'd been reduced to taping her nightly newscasts on his VCR, then watching a whole week's worth on Sundays, the only day of the week he didn't spend slaving at his desk. Sometimes he'd watch the tape over and over again, trying to decipher what she was thinking as she capably explained the day's events.

He wondered how she was doing. He wondered if she'd gotten over the disappointment of losing that network slot. He wondered if she was lonely, too.

He wondered if she'd found someone else.

To be on the safe side, he shoved two more antacids into his mouth. It was going to be another long afternoon. He only wished he didn't anticipate a lifetime of equally long afternoons in front of him.

"YOU LOOK LIKE hell, buddy." Todd Sinewski's blunt assessment only confirmed Cliff's own impression.

He'd answered the pounding on his front door with wildly beating heart. Maybe Mallory had had second thoughts. Maybe she was sorry she'd deserted him. Maybe—maybe it's only Todd at the door.

Disappointed, he turned away, a movement that allowed Todd to push his way inside and close the door.

''What the hell's wrong with you, Cliff? You look worse than the bum I gave a dollar to yesterday in the Gaslamp Quarter.''

He shrugged. ''I quit my job.''

''I heard.'' Todd settled down on the large leather sofa. ''Do you want to tell me why?''

Cliff shrugged and reached for the remote. He'd just started playing this week's tape when Todd's pounding interrupted his obsessive viewing.

''You look like you haven't shaved in a week.''

''I haven't. Or maybe longer. I don't remember.''

''Your hair needs a trim.''

''So?'' He pressed the start button on the remote, then used fast forward to whiz past the various commercials.

''Your cutoffs have definitely seen better days and could use a wash.'' Todd gave an indelicate sniff. ''And so could you, from the smell of it.''

''Get to the point.'' Cliff was barely listening. His attention was focused on the cool blonde on the screen. She had her hair down. He'd always liked it down.

"Will you give me that!" Todd snatched the remote and turned the tape and television off.

"Hey!"

"I'm not letting you go back to your wallowing until you tell me what's going on. Why has the city's most ambitious overachiever turned into a couch potato?"

Cliff's eyes, red-rimmed and burning, met Todd's gaze. "God's truth, Todd, I have no idea. One day I was kicking along just fine, well on the way to a partnership. The next thing I know, I hate my job, and I'm obsessing over a woman who loves me but doesn't want me anywhere around her."

"Mallory Reissen?" Todd gestured to the screen.

"Uh-huh." Suddenly, the words poured out. Cliff explained the whole sorry mess—the affair that was supposed to solve all his problems and how it had only created one larger than anything he'd ever dealt with in his life.

Todd listened in silence. Finally, after Cliff ran out of words, he said, "You say she said she loves you. Yet she doesn't want you to work so hard?"

"That's about the size of it. I tell you, Todd, I've just about gone crazy over her. I don't know what I'm doing anymore."

''Well, quitting your job doesn't seem to be a real bright move.''

Cliff shrugged. ''I haven't really quit. Just taken a leave of absence.''

''In the middle of the biggest trial to hit San Diego? When you're on the defense team? *Are you nuts?*''

Cliff met his gaze straight on. ''Maybe. Probably.'' He took a deep breath. ''But you know what? I really *hate* being a big-time defense attorney. The clients are so slimy. If you know what I mean.''

''Yeah, I got it.'' Todd took a deep breath. ''You know, I never thought I'd live to see this happen to you. But I think you *are* nuts—nuts about Mallory Reissen. Maybe you should think about doing something about it.''

''You think I haven't tried? She won't take my calls. She's virtually disappeared from her condo—I haven't seen her go in or out of there in weeks. About the only thing left for me to try is to lay siege to her at work—and if she really has gotten over me, that would humiliate her and me.''

''It's a problem all right,'' Todd admitted.

''I'm in love with her, you know. It took a long time for me to realize it—too long. Now I can't even get her to listen to me long enough to try to apologize.''

"Is this how you've been spending your time? Watching tapes of her over and over?"

"Pretty much. Wanna help me watch?"

Taking Todd's silence as acceptance, Cliff picked up the remote and turned the television and VCR back on. Silently, they watched the week's newscasts together, with Cliff fast-forwarding past anything that didn't have Mallory on screen.

It didn't take long for them to get to Friday's broadcast. At the very end of the program, the camera focused in on Mallory. Cliff caught his breath. How could he have been so stupid as to let her go? More to the point, how could he get her back?

On the screen, Mallory was talking. "—and I'd like to take a moment in my final broadcast here in San Diego to thank all the wonderful people in the city and especially here at KSAN television. It'll be a wrench leaving you all, but I'd like to wish everyone here in San Diego a happy, healthy life. Thank you for all your support." A tear glimmered in her eyes. "Goodbye. This is Mallory Reissen, signing off."

Stunned, Cliff turned to Todd. "Did you hear what I did? Did she just say that she'd left the station?"

Todd nodded. "That's what it sounded like to me."

Cliff picked up the telephone and punched in the number he knew by heart. Her office number rang and rang, until a taped voice came on the line and said, "You have reached an extension that is not currently in use. Please redial, or press 0 to reach the operator."

The operator confirmed that Mallory Reissen no longer worked at KSAN television, but could not—or would not—say where she had gone.

His hands shaking, Cliff punched in her home phone number. This time the recorded voice came on after only two rings. "The number you have dialed has been disconnected."

Without bothering to explain to Todd, he dashed out the front door and to hers next door. For the first time he noticed a small, discreet For Sale sign posted in the niche by her door. And when he peered through the now-curtainless window, he saw that no furniture remained inside.

Sometime recently she'd moved out.

Todd found him there moments later, sitting on the front doorstep, bitter tears etching his cheeks. In despair he looked up. "I've lost her, Todd. She's gone."

MALLORY SMILED up at the warm Sierra sunshine, her arms full of groceries. She'd been in Sunfield for three weeks and still enjoyed every moment. The small town was just as she remembered it from her childhood, filled with gentle people and a charming, low-key life-style. She woke each morning in her grandmother's house, trying hard to think only of her contentment in her new life, trying hard to forget that she'd left her heart behind in San Diego.

Every so often she wondered how he was doing. He'd wrapped himself so firmly around her heart that she knew she'd never break free of him. Nor did she want to. She treasured every moment of their loving. If remembrances were all she could have of him, remembrances would be what she'd make do with.

The nights were lonely, of course, and sometimes she would see a dark-haired man from a distance and feel her heartbeat accelerate.

It had all seemed so clear to her. When she realized she had to give up her relationship with Cliff, she recognized at last that she'd spent twenty-eight years striving for a crumb of appreciation from parents who simply didn't care.

She didn't really want that New York job—or at least she could live without it. What she wanted was a meaningful life with neighbors and a job she really loved, not one she did merely to impress her parents. She wanted children, too—PTA meetings and school plays and Jimmy-pushed-me-Mom squabbles. Most of all, she wanted to find a man just like Cliff, but one who also was willing to give up the ''good'' life of ambition for the even better life of love and family.

In the depths of the night when tears and longing were her only companions, she knew it would take her a long time to get over losing Cliff, but she had to try. For her own happiness, she had to forget him.

She'd had no choice except to leave him. She refused to let herself become one more woman he wanted to forget. He knew she loved him—she was glad of that. But her heartache and longing for him was private, not to be cheapened by painful scenes.

And she loved her new life. When she'd looked for a way to escape, she'd remembered the small college in the slightly larger town next to Sunfield. The communications department had been thrilled with her proposal to teach radio and television technology to their students. She was already looking forward to the start of classes in the fall.

She took her time as she walked the quarter mile back to her grandmother's house—*her* house now. There was no hurry; none of her groceries would spoil. And the day was beautiful—warm sunshine with just enough breeze to remind her she was in the mountains. As usual, her eyes drank in the picturesque setting eagerly, lingering on a quarrelsome squirrel here, a sassy mountain bluebird there.

So she was almost on top of the gold-colored Lexus before she noticed it.

*His* car.

Her steps slowed to a halt beside the front fender as she looked toward the front porch of her house.

"Hello, Mallory."

Her arms loosened and would have dropped the groceries if he hadn't stepped down from the porch and collected the bags. He set them on the porch, then took her arm and guided her to the swing suspended from the porch ceiling.

"Are you all right?" he asked solicitously.

"Cliff?" To her dismay, every nerve in her body seemed to have migrated to her elbow, directly underneath his protective hand. "What are you doing here?"

He shrugged, but his intense gaze belied the gesture. "Looking for you."

"How did you find me?"

His irises gleamed an intense pewter, a sign of some deep feeling held in check. Sunlight glinted off his dark auburn hair, but she noticed one or two silvery strands. And the tiny lines at the corners of his eyes seemed deeper.

"It wasn't easy. All I could remember was that your grandmother's house was in Sun-something. Do you know how many small towns in the Sierras start with 'Sun'?"

She shook her head, noticing the faint crease between his brows.

"Well, there are a ton of them. I had to check out

every one individually. Naturally, Sunfield was almost at the bottom of my list.''

"You found me, though.'' She started to reach out to him, then checked the gesture.

"Yes,'' he said, and even she couldn't miss the satisfaction in that word. "I found you.''

"You're...looking good.'' Actually, he looked fabulous, though very tired. With an effort, she kept her fingers from smoothing the lines of weariness from his brow. Even his suit and tieless shirt seemed somehow appropriate for him, although he was the first person she'd seen in a suit since she'd hit town.

"You too,'' he said. From the way his eyes inspected every inch of her sundress-clad body, bare legs, and sandaled feet, she knew it was no casual compliment.

She tore her gaze from him and focused on the huge pine across the street. "Cliff, why are you here? Is the Bartlett trial over?'' He heart hammered in her chest with hopes that suddenly, desperately tried to fly free.

He shrugged again. "I don't know. I quit my job.''

That drew her attention. "What? *Why?*''

"Because I realized I hated my work.'' He paused. "Mallory, this can't be a surprise to you. We talked about how different it was from what I expected when we were up in that cabin in Julian, remember?''

"But—to give up your ambitions—I can't believe it."

"Mallory, my ambitions were making me ill. You were right about that, too. My doctor told me I was well on the way to building a dandy ulcer. I realized after you left that I was still trying to impress a ten-year-old kid from the wrong side of the tracks. My career was more for the kid I used to be, not for the adult I am now."

"Like me trying to impress my parents, instead of doing what I really wanted," she murmured.

His eyes lasered into hers. "And what is it you really do want? I thought it was a network job in New York."

Mallory's breath caught. She should have known he'd ask. Carefully, she kept her eyes on his hands, not quite willing to meet his gaze. "I realized I want something different from my parents. They wanted to prove themselves to the whole world."

"And you don't?"

She smiled a little wistfully. "Not really. I'll be happy if I can prove myself to myself. And maybe…"

"Maybe?"

"Maybe to someone else, too. Cliff, why are you here?"

A knot of tension visibly eased in his shoulders. "Because you're here," he said gently. He took her hand and a fortifying breath. "I wanted to ask you a question."

"What question?" Those hopes were beginning to flutter into her throat. It was hard to force her words past them.

"How do you feel about unemployment?"

"What?" Of all the possible questions she'd breathlessly imagined he might ask, that wasn't one of them.

"Well, you see before you a guy with no job. I sold my condo—and at a cut-rate price, I might add, because someone else had recently put hers on the market, driving up the supply."

Her hand turned, weaving her fingers with his. The thudding of her heart almost drowned his soft words.

"Where was I? Oh, yes. No job. No home. I sold all my too-expensive furniture. Just a used car and some clothes to call my own."

"A used *Lexus*," she pointed out helpfully.

"Yeah. You know how expensive those are to insure and maintain? Like I said, a used car." He took a deep breath and leaned his forehead against hers. "So what do you think? Do my reduced circumstances put me completely out of the running?"

Her free hand traced the creases of his cheek. Her heart was thudding so powerfully, she could barely squeeze out a reply. "Out of the running for what? I understand Sunfield needs a new dogcatcher."

He shook his head. "Nope. I'm allergic."

"Oh. Well, what did you have in mind?"

"Maybe a small practice here. I used to be a pretty good lawyer, you know. And a proposition, really. Sort of like the one you once made me."

She groaned. "Not another great-sex-and-no-commitments affair!"

"Not a chance. How about great-sex-and-lots-of-commitments? How about you marry me and put me out of my misery? And then we'll talk about our affairs."

His suggestion sent her temper soaring. "You will *not* have affairs while you're my husband! No way!"

"Sure I will—with you. I figure if an affair is what you want, an affair is what you'll get. But only if you marry me first."

"And what if I want more?"

He watched her warily. "What do you mean by more?"

She took a deep breath. "Children. A family. What if I want that, too?"

His head lifted from hers and the wariness was back in his eyes. "Children? Mallory…you're not…"

She shook her head. "No, I'm not pregnant. Not yet, anyway." Her eyes searched his. "But would it be so awful if I were?"

"Pregnant…" He tasted the word slowly and the

thoughtful gleam in his eye worried her. His hand slipped down her neck to settle on her stomach in a protective caress. "My baby growing inside you…no, 'awful' isn't exactly how I'd describe that."

"How—how would you describe it?" Her hopes had reached her mouth and eyes, curving her lips into a smile and bringing the sting of joyous tears to her eyes.

"Heaven on earth. Mallory, marry me. Have my babies. Make me complete."

The smile on her face must have outshone the sun because she saw its light reflected in his eyes. Deliberately, she tried to lighten her voice. "Sounds like an okay deal to me. But, Counselor, shouldn't we negotiate some more?"

"Negotiate what?"

"Well, you haven't told me you love me yet. Seems to me that's an essential part of the deal."

"Oh. Well, maybe you're right."

He slipped to his knees beside the swing and pulled a small box out of his pants pocket. "I love you, Mallory Reissen, more than I ever thought I could love someone else. Please marry me." He opened the box and offered her a simple solitaire diamond that was not ostentatiously large, but perfectly shaped for her hand.

Gracefully she let him slip it on her finger, then

she slipped to her knees facing him. "I love you too, Cliff. I told you so weeks ago and every day apart has only made that love deeper and more a part of me. I could live without you, I'm sure. But I can't be joyful without you. I can't have the love I need without you."

His arms slipped around her and hugged her tightly against him. "Ah, Mallory, Mallory. How much I love you!"

For long moments, they stayed there, luxuriating in the simple pleasure of holding each other in their arms. Finally, Cliff said, "Uh, Mallory?"

"What?" Her lips had already started to explore his cheek.

"Could we get up? My knees are killing me."

With a burble of laughter, she helped her complaining lover up.

"Do I take it that we're in agreement at last?" he asked as she guided him toward her front door and more private—and comfortable—surroundings.

"Maybe," she said, pretending to ponder. "We've certainly adjusted the terms of our affair to some that are more to my liking."

His arm curled around her, he headed up the stairs. "Yeah. As I recall, we originally wanted an affair with great sex and no commitments."

She pointed out the door to her bedroom. "And

now we've got a great-sex-and-profound-commit-ments affair.''

He turned her to face him and looked into her eyes with an intensity and sincerity she couldn't miss. ''No, Mallory. Now we've got a love that will last a lifetime. Now we've got a marriage. And we're go-ing to have a marriage and a family. And that makes all the difference.''

Mallory could only agree happily with his assess-ment of their circumstances. Love did make the dif-ference. And she intended to spend a lifetime show-ing him—and herself—just how much a difference it made.

# MILLS & BOON®

*Makes any time special*™

## Mills & Boon publish 29 new titles every month. Select from...

Modern Romance™     Tender Romance™

Sensual Romance™

Medical Romance™   Historical Romance™

MAT2

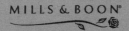

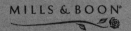

MILLS & BOON®

# Modern Romance™

## *THE PREGNANT BRIDE* by *Catherine Spencer*

Jenna Sinclair couldn't regret her passion-filled night with stranger, Edmund Delaney—and when she told Edmund she was pregnant he appeared far from dismayed. It seemed he had his own agenda…

## *THE TYCOON'S MISTRESS* by *Sara Craven*

Cressy was astonished when Draco Viannis proposed. Surely they were just having a passionate holiday affair? When Cressy returned home to find her family in crisis, only Draco could help—for a price. And the price was Cressy in his bed once more…

## *THE ITALIAN GROOM* by *Jane Porter*

Meg had returned to her Californian hometown in an effort to come to terms with her future as a single mother. But family friend Niccolo Dominico insisted that he should take care of her and her baby—and that meant marriage!

## *BACHELOR BOSS* by *Pamela Ingrahm*

Philip Ambercroft prized efficiency, order, and no temptation in the office. He was determined to deny his attraction to his new temporary assistant Madalyn Weir—he was *not* prepared to propose a marriage merger…was he?

## On sale 2nd February 2001

0101/01b

0102/98/MB10
MILLS & BOON
THIS TIME...
MARRIAGE
Three brides get the chance to make it This Time... Forever.
Great value—
3 compelling novels in 1.
Available from 2nd February 2001

# 4 FREE
## books and a surprise gift!

We would like to take this opportunity to thank you for reading this Mills & Boon® book by offering you the chance to take FOUR more specially selected titles from the Modern Romance™ series absolutely FREE! We're also making this offer to introduce you to the benefits of the Reader Service™—

- ★ FREE home delivery
- ★ FREE gifts and competitions
- ★ FREE monthly Newsletter
- ★ Exclusive Reader Service discounts
- ★ Books available before they're in the shops

Accepting these FREE books and gift places you under no obligation to buy, you may cancel at any time, even after receiving your free shipment. Simply complete your details below and return the entire page to the address below. *You don't even need a stamp!*

**YES!** Please send me 4 free Modern Romance books and a surprise gift. I understand that unless you hear from me, I will receive 6 superb new titles every month for just £2.40 each, postage and packing free. I am under no obligation to purchase any books and may cancel my subscription at any time. The free books and gift will be mine to keep in any case.

P1ZEA

Ms/Mrs/Miss/Mr ..............................Initials......................................
BLOCK CAPITALS PLEASE

Surname ...............................................................................................

Address ................................................................................................

.............................................................................................................

.................................................................Postcode ...............................

**Send this whole page to:**
**UK: FREEPOST CN81, Croydon, CR9 3WZ**
**EIRE: PO Box 4546, Kilcock, County Kildare (stamp required)**